George White

Memoir of His Eminence Cardinal Wiseman

First Archbishop of Westminster, &c. With portrait and autography.

George White

Memoir of His Eminence Cardinal Wiseman
First Archbishop of Westminster, &c. With portrait and autography.

ISBN/EAN: 9783337310752

Printed in Europe, USA, Canada, Australia, Japan

Cover: Foto ©Raphael Reischuk / pixelio.de

More available books at **www.hansebooks.com**

MEMOIR

OF HIS EMINENCE

CARDINAL WISEMAN,

First Archbishop of Westminster.

&c. &c.

With Portrait and Autograph.

LONDON:
RICHARDSON AND SON,
PATERNOSTER ROW; DUBLIN, AND DERBY.

1865.

MEMOIR.

NEARLY a century has elapsed since the first attempt was made by the Legislature of England to relieve the Catholics of this country from the penal laws under which they had been oppressed since the "Reformation." The Relief Bill was followed by a storm of popular frenzy and violence, and the Metropolis was for some days delivered up to mob law. It seemed almost hopeless to expect that any further measures would be taken to grant civil rights to the depressed and insignificant body who still remained firm in their attachment to the old faith. At this juncture the Almighty's scourge fell upon a neighbouring nation, and England, who ignored and oppressed her Catholic subjects at home, opened wide her arms to receive the bands of foreign professors of that faith who fled from the tyranny of an infidel oligarchy. In return for this hospitality shown to hundreds of pious, learned, and zealous ecclesiastics, the Almighty would seem to have chosen them to commence the great work of rekindling the faith in this country, which had been brought to our Saxon forefathers by the Roman Augustine at the word of Pope Gregory. While the French refugees were at their holy labours, from the mansions of the noble and wealthy to the obscure alleys of our cities and towns, Divine Providence called forth a child from a famed city of the distant peninsula to return to the land of his fathers to prepare to take his part in the great religious revival of the commencement of the century, and to become at the middle of it the first Primate of the restored hierarchy. This child—the subject of this memoir—was Nicholas Wiseman, son of the late James Wiseman, merchant, of Waterford and of Seville, in which latter city he was born on the 2nd of August, 1802. The family of Wiseman is one of considerable antiquity, and they appear to have had lands in the county of Essex since the reign of Edward IV. Soon after the "Reformation" Sir John Wiseman, who had been one of the Auditors of the Exchequer under Henry VIII., and was

knighted for his bravery at the battle of Spurs, acquired by
purchase, Much Canfield Park in that county.   His grandson,
William, who married into the noble family of Capel, afterwards Earl of Essex, was created a Barouet by King Charles
I. in 1628, and a younger brother of the second Baronet was
Bishop of Dromore.   The title has continued in a direct line
of succession down to the present time, and is now represented
by Sir William Saltonstall Wiseman, eighth baronet, who is a
captain in the Royal Navy.   From a younger branch of this
family the late Cardinal traditionally claimed descent.   His
mother, Xaviera, was daughter of the late Peter Strange,
Esq., whose family, in spite of large confiscations of their
property under Oliver Cromwell, is still settled at Aylward's
Town Castle, in the county of Kilkenny, and was nearly
related to the late Lady Bellew.   The branch of Mrs. Wiseman's family settled in Spain was long and well known to the
great banking and mercantile houses of London.   Their uncle,
Mr. L. Strange, of Cadiz, was not more prized by them than
the eminent house of Wiseman Brothers of Seville.   When,
during the frenzy which succeeded the establishment of the
hierarchy, the fair fame of his mother was most dastardly
attacked, the Cardinal wrote:—" I have for the last two
months borne silently much calumny and railing against myself,
and I am ready to go on enduring personally more still for
what I believe to be the cause of God ; but I cannot allow to
pass unnoticed any slander of one to whom I owe all good in
life, and whom God's commandments enjoin me to honour,
and consequently to shield from dishonour.   Although nearly
an octogenarian, my venerable parent retains still full
possession of every faculty, and a keen sense of honour,
having passed her days with the respect and esteem of all
that knew her."   The good lady did not long survive her
son's elevation to the Cardinalate, but died on the 7th Feb.,
1851—the very day on which the futile Ecclesiastical Titles
Act was introduced into the House of Commons.

Nicholas, having lost his father while very young, was
naturally brought by his mother to her own friends and
country.   They landed at Portsmouth in January, 1808,
and, after a short stay in London, proceeded to Aylward's
Town, near Waterford, at a boarding school in which city
Nicholas learned the first rudiments of his mother tongue " as
completely as a child could learn it."   But as England was

to be the scene of his future labours and triumphs, so in it was he destined to receive the ground-work of that learning and science in which he was so highly to excel. At the breaking out of the French Revolutionary war at the close of the last century, the English Catholic College at Douai was early seized upon by the Republican army, and the Professors and Students who had not already fled from the approaching storm were sent to prison, whence, however, they mostly escaped, and arrived safely in England about the year 1794. Shortly after their arrival, they established themselves at Crook Hall, an ancient seat of the Baker family, about ten miles from the city of Durham. This building, was, however, soon found to be totally inadequate to supply the exigencies of the Northern District (now the Diocese of Hexham), when the late Bishop Gibson conceived the bold design of forming an establishment on a much more extensive scale, and, supported by the liberal donations and co-operation of the Clergy and Laity of the district, was enabled to carry this undertaking to a successful issue. The site of the College of Ushaw (dedicated to St. Cuthbert), with about 250 acres of land, he purchased from Sir Edward Smythe, Bart., of Acton Burnel, Salop. In 1804 the building was commenced, and in four years was ready for the reception of students.

To this College was Nicholas Wiseman brought by his mother, who settled at Durham to be near her son, in case of his needing her maternal care. At Ushaw began the Cardinal's acquaintance with the Rev. Mr. (afterwards Dr.) Lingard, who was Vice-President of the College. Of this distinguished scholar His Eminence writes:—"I have retained upon my memory the vivid recollection of specific acts of thoughtful and delicate kindness, which showed a tender heart mindful of its duties amidst the many harassing occupations just devolved on him through the death of the President (Rev. Thos. Eyre), and his own literary engagements; for he was re-conducting his first great work (on the Anglo-Saxon Church) through the press. But though he went from College soon after, and I later left the country, and saw him not again for fifteen years, yet there grew up an indirect understanding first and by degrees a correspondence, and an intimacy which continued to the close of his life." At Ushaw the young Nicholas felt the first signs of that "vocation" to the ecclesiastical state which is so all important in the eyes of Catholics, and without which no Catholic would dare to thrust himself into the sanctuary. After going through his humanities with great honours and success, his superiors fixed upon him to be one of six youths who were to be sent to revive the English College in Rome.

The foundation of this institution dates from the time of the Saxon King Ina, who opened a home for his countrymen visiting the shrine of the Apostles. "Still (to continue in the Cardinal's own words) nothing like an *hospice* for English pilgrims existed till the first great Jubilee, when John Shepherd and his wife Alice seeing this want settled in Rome, and devoted their substance to the support of poor palmers from their own country. This small beginning grew into sufficient importance for it to become a royal charity; the king of England became its patron and named its rector, often a person of high consideration.

" In the archives of the college are preserved the lists of the pilgrims who from year to year visited Rome; and as the country or diocese from which they came is recorded, it is a valuable document often consulted for local or family history. Many of the pilgrims were youths of good connections, students of Bologna, who in their holidays, or at the close of their course, chose to visit Rome *in formâ pauperum*, and received hospitality in the 'English Hospital of St. Thomas.'

" The rupture of Henry VIII. with the Holy See put an end to the influx of pilgrims from England to Rome, and arrivals pretty nearly ceased under Elizabeth. In the meantime, three different English establishments had been united—those of the Holy Trinity, of St. Thomas, and of St. Edward—on the spot where the present College stands; and a church had been built, the great altar-piece of which, yet preserved, commemorated the formation of this coalition. A Bishop and several other refugees for the faith lived there till Gregory XIII., in 1579, converted the hospital into a college, as then more needed, with the condition that should the religious position of England ever change, the institution should return to its original purpose. May the happy omen be accomplished, but without any necessity for its proposed consequence."

The account given by the Cardinal himself of the voyage to Leghorn and its attendant perils, will show how clearly Divine Providence watched over a life so precious in His eyes, and destined to work out His blessings upon the English nation :—"It was on the 18th of December, 1818, that I arrived in Rome, in company with five other youths sent to colonise the English College in that city, after it had been desolate and uninhabited during almost the period of a generation. It was long before a single steamer had appeared in the Mediterranean, or even plied between the French and English coasts. The land journey across France, over the Alps, and down Italy was then a formidable undertaking, and required appliances, personal and material, scarcely compatible with the purposes of their journey. A voyage by sea from Liverpool to Leghorn was, therefore, considered the simplest method of conveying a party of ten persons from England to Italy. The embarkation took place on the 2nd of October, and the arrival late in December. During this period a fortnight was spent in beating up from Savona to Genoa, another week in running from Genoa to Livorno; a man fell overboard and was drowned off Cape St. Vincent; a dog went raving mad on board from want of fresh water, and luckily, after clearing the decks jumped or slipped into the sea; the vessel was once at least on fire; and all the passengers were nearly lost in a sudden squall in Ramsay Bay, into which they had been driven by stress of weather, and where they of course landed: and the reader, who may now make the whole journey in four days, will indulgently understand how pleasing must have been to those early travellers' ears the usual indication, by voice and outstretched whip, embodied in the well-known exclamation of every *vetturino*, 'Ecco Roma.'

"Having come so far, somewhat in the spirit of sacrifice, in some expectation of having to 'rough it,' as pioneers for less venturesome followers, it seemed incredible that we should have fallen upon such pleasant places as the seat of future life and occupation. One felt at once at home; it was nobody else's house; it was English ground, a part of our fatherland, a restored inheritance. And though, indeed, all was neat and trim, dazzling in its whiteness, relieved here and there by tinted architectural members, one could not but feel that we had been transported to the scene of better men and greater things than were likely to arise in the new era that day opened. Just within the great entrance door, a small one to the right led into the old church of the Holy Trinity, which wanted but its roof to restore it to use. There it stood, nave and aisle, separated by pillars connected by arches, all in their places, with the lofty walls above them.   The altars had been, indeed, removed; but we could trace their forms, and the painted walls marked the frames of the altar-pieces, especially of the noble painting by Durante Alberti, still preserved in the house, representing the Patron-Mystery, and St. Thomas of Canterbury, and St. Edward the Martyr.

"The re-establishment of the suppressed English College in Rome, was the work almost spontaneous of Pius VII. and of his great minister Cardinal Consalvi.

"Although a rector, and one qualified for his office, had been in possession of the house for a year, the arrival of a colony of students was the real opening of the establishment. On the day alluded to, the excellent superior, the Rev. Robert Gradwell, on returning home, found the first instalment of this important body really installed in his house, to the extent of having converted to present use the preparations for his own frugal and solitary meal.

"The event was of sufficient magnitude to be communicated to the Secretary of State; and the answer was, that as many of the party as could be provided with the old and hallowed costume of the English College, should be presented to the Holy Father (Pius VII.) within a few days.   Among the more fortunate ones, owing to a favourable accident, was myself.

"It will be easily conceived that our hearts beat with more than usual speed, and not without some little flurry, as we ascended the great staircase of the Quirinal palace on Christmas-eve, the day appointed for audience.   After a short delay, we were summoned to enter a room, so small that it scarcely allowed space for the usual genuflections at the door, and in the middle of the apartment.   But instead of receiving us, as was customary, seated, the mild and amiable Pontiff had risen to welcome us, and meet us as we approached.   He did not allow it to be a mere presentation— it was a fatherly reception, and in the truest sense our inauguration into the duties that awaited us.   It will be best, however, to give the particulars of this first interview with the occupant of St. Peter's Chair, in the words of a memorandum entered, probably that day, in the Rector's Journal. 'December 24.   Took six of the students to the Pope.   The other four could not be clothed.   The Holy Father received them standing, shook hands with each, and welcomed them to Rome.   He praised the English clergy for their good and peaceful conduct, and their fidelity to the Holy See. He exhorted the youths to learning and piety, and said, "I hope you will do honour both to Rome, and to your own country."

That expression was not thrown away upon Nicholas Wiseman. It was seed cast upon fertile ground. From that time it incited him to renewed efforts to advance the interests of the Catholic Church, and to do what he thought would benefit England, his adopted country. He studied hard and soon attracted attention. When he was eighteen years of age he published his first book. It was entitled, "Horæ Syriacæ," and was a treatise on Oriental languages—a study in which he was intensely interested. Before he was ordained priest he had obtained the degree of D.D. by a public defension. As soon as he was twenty-three years of age he was ordained priest, that being the earliest age at which the Catholic Church allows ordination to the priesthood. His extraordinary abilities were known to the Pope and the College of Cardinals, and he was not allowed to return to England at once, but was created a professor of the Roman University.

In 1827 Dr. Wiseman received an order from Leo XII. to preach a course of sermons in one of the large Churches of Rome, from Advent to Lent. It is most interesting to hear the Cardinal's own reflections on this command, as doubtless on it depended his Eminence's future celebrity as a preacher, and more particularly a lecturer.

"His Holiness remarked, that there being no English Churches in Rome, Catholics who came there had no opportunity of hearing the word of God, and even others who might desire to hear a sermon in their own language, had no means of gratifying their wish. It was, therefore, he said, his intention to have, during the winter, in some church well-situated, a course of English sermons, to be delivered every Sunday. It was to be attended by all colleges and religious communities that spoke our language. However, the burthen was laid there and then with peremptory kindness, by an authority that might not be gainsaid. And crushingly it pressed upon the shoulders : it would be impossible to describe the anxiety, pain, and trouble which this command cost for many years after. Leo could not see what has been the influence of his commission, in merely dragging from the commerce with the dead, to that of the living, one who would gladly have confined his time to the former—from books to men, from reading to speaking. Nothing but this would have done it. Yet supposing that the providence of one's life was to be active, and in contact with the world, and one's future duties were to be in a country, and in times where the most bashful may be driven to plead for his religion or his flock, surely a command, over-riding all inclination, and forcing the will to undertake the best and only preparation for these tasks, may well be contemplated as a sacred impulse, and a timely direction to a mind that wanted both. Had it not come then it never more could have come; other bents would soon have become stiffened and impliant; and no second opportunity could have been opened, after others had satisfied the first demand. One may, therefore, feel grateful for the gracious severity of that day, and the more in proportion to what it cost; for what was then done was spared one later.

"He (Leo XII.) selected a church of most just proportions for the work, and of exquisite beauty, that of Gesù e Maria in the Corso; he had it furnished at his own expense each Sunday; he ordered all charges for advertisements, and other costs, to be defrayed by the palace, or civil list; and what was more useful and considerate than all, a detachment of his own choir attended, to introduce the service by its own peculiar music. Its able director, Canonico Baini, the closest approximator, in modern times, to Palestrina and Bai, composed a little mottet, with English words, for our special use."

After Lent, fatigued and almost broken down by new anxious labours and insomnium, Dr. Wiseman "started for Naples and Sicily; travelled round that island when it had only twelve miles of carriage road in it; ascended not only Vesuvius, but to the crater of Etna; encountered only trifling but characteristic adventures sufficient to amuse friends; and returned with new vigour home, to find our dear and venerable Rector (Dr. Gradwell) appointed Bishop, and about to leave Rome for ever.

"On the 6th December, 1828, I received the last mark of kindness and confidence from our Holy Pontiff, in the nomination to the vacated office (rectorship), and had subsequently my last audience of thanks, fatherly, and encouraging as usual."

In the meantime the English legislature were driven by O'Connell to grant the Catholics of these kingdoms that freedom for religious worship which had so long and so cruelly been refused them. Of this event the Cardinal writes: "Pius

VIII. was elected March 31, 1829, and, scarcely a month later, it was my pleasing duty to communicate to him the gladsome tidings of Catholic Emancipation. This great and just measure received the royal assent on the 23rd of April following. It need hardly be remarked, that such a message was one of unbounded joy, and might well have been communicated to the head of the Catholic Church in the words by which the arrival of paschal time is announced to him every year : '*Pater sancte, annuntio vobis gaudium magnum.*' After audience of the Pope, the Vice Rector of the College (now Archbishop of Trebizonde) and myself visited the Secretary of State and received from him warm expressions of congratulation. We then proceeded to make preparations for our festival on the usual Roman plan. The front of our house was covered with an elegant architectural design in variegated lamps, and an orchestra was erected opposite for festive music. In the morning .of the appointed day, a *Te Deum*, attended by the various British Colleges, was performed ; in the afternoon a banquet on a munificent scale was given at his villa near St. Paul's, by Monsignor Nicolai, the learned illustrator of that Basilica ; and in the evening we returned home to see the upturned faces of multitudes reflecting the brilliant ' lamps of architecture ' that tapestried our venerable walls, with the words ' Emancipazione Cattolica ' which were emblazoned in lamps along the front."

In Lent, 1835, Dr. Wiseman delivered his famous lectures on the " Connection between Science and Revealed Religion." Of these lectures he says in the preface to the first edition, that they were " first drawn up for private instruction and read by me in the English College at Rome, over which I had the honour of presiding, being intended for an introductory course to the study of theology. At the request of several friends I was induced to deliver them to a public audience, and during the Lent of 1835 they were read to a large and select attendance in the apartments of his Eminence Cardinal Weld." Of these lectures the Cardinal thus writes :—" A few years ago, I prefixed to a thesis held by a member of the English College (afterwards Bishop Baggs,) a Latin dissertation of ten or twelve pages, upon the necessity of uniting general and scientific knowledge to theological pursuits. I took a rapid view of the different branches of learning discussed in these Lectures. The essay was soon translated into Italian and printed in a Sicilian journal; and I believe appeared also at Milan. What was most gratifying to my own feelings, and may serve as a confirmation of the assertions in the text, is, that when two days after, I waited upon the late Pope Pius VIII., a man truly well versed in sacred and profane literature, to present him according to usage with a copy of the thesis prepared for him, I found him with it on his table; and in the kindest terms, he informed me, that, having heard of my little Essay, he had instantly sent for it, and added, ' You have robbed Egypt of its spoil, and shown that it belongs to the people of God.'"

It has been generally, but erroneously stated, that in 1835 Dr. Wiseman "was summoned to London for missionary duties." The only actual experience of the mission the late Cardinal had, was at the Royal Sardinian Chapel (now S.S. Anselm and Cecilia's), Lincoln's Inn Fields. The head Priest of that chapel, the Rev. A. M. Baldacconi, D.D. (now of Gosport), wishing to pay a visit to his family in Italy, induced his friend Dr. Wiseman to take charge of his mission during his absence, on account of the Italian portion of the congregation, to whom the late Cardinal preached every Sunday afternoon, with an ease and fluency that made strangers who heard him take him for an Italian. It was during this period that the writer of this memoir had the honour and happiness to become acquainted with Dr. Wiseman.

It was at the Royal Sardinian Chapel, then subsidized by the good Charles Albert, that Dr. Wiseman delivered a course of Lectures during the Advent of 1835. The great success of these discourses, induced Bishop Bramstone, V.A. of the London District, to request the learned divine to deliver his celebrated "Lectures on the doctrines of the Catholic Church," at St Mary's, Moorfields. "Dr. Wiseman's Moorfields Lectures are known to every English reader, whether Catholic or Protestant, who takes any interest in theological controversy. Society in this country was surprised, and listened almost against its will, and listened not displeased. Here was a young Roman Priest, fresh from the centre of Catholicism, who showed himself master not only of the intricacies of polemical discussion, but also of the amenities of civilized life. Protestants were equally astonished and gratified to find that acuteness and urbanity were not incompatible even in controversial argument. The spacious church of Moorfields was thronged on every evening of Dr. Wiseman's appearance in its pulpit (it is said that one or more members of the Royal Family were present at them), many persons of position and education were converted, and all departed with abated prejudice, and with very different notions about Catholicism from those with which they had been prepossessed by their education. A certain number of excellent Priests now labouring in our midst might be named, who are the sons of men converted by Dr. Wiseman, during these lectures."

Of the conversions which took place this year, was that of one who was destined to play no small part in the work of building up and reviving the material Church in this land. This was Augustus Welby Pugin. He attributed his conversion, in part at least, to Dr. Wiseman's writings. No one, perhaps, better than the late Cardinal, educated as he was amidst the splendours of Papal Rome, estimated at its true value the importance of the restoration of the ancient style of architecture, so deeply implanted in the minds of all Englishmen in connection with the ancient faith of the land.

In the same year (1836), Dr. Wiseman, in conjunction with Mr. O'Connell and Mr. Quin, established the *Dublin Review*, and was for some time joint-editor of that work, which at once took, and has since retained a high place among the leading Reviews of the kingdom. In the first number, Dr. Wiseman wrote an article on the "Oxford Controversy," and later, a series on the "High Church Claims," which were then being put forward by the Oxford party. The Cardinal continued to write for this Review, articles not only on the great religious questions of the day (one on the Donatists, is said to have been a great means of bringing Dr. Newman into the Church), but also on matters connected with church discipline, the ritual, art, and foreign travel. His chief contributions to the *Dublin Review* were collected and published in three volumes a few years ago. In 1839, the six articles on "High Church Claims" were reprinted, and very widely disseminated as tracts by the "Catholic Institute of Great Britain." Dr. Wiseman also wrote, at the solicitation of Mr. C. Knight, the article on the "Catholic Church" for the "Penny Cyclopædia."

Dr. Wiseman again visited England in July 1839, and went about preaching and lecturing, chiefly in the Midland Counties. A cotemporary review announced that "from the

end of July to November this indefatigable ecclesiastic
travelled upwards of 2000 miles, and preached and lectured
upwards of 100 times." During this time Dr. Wiseman
preached the Retreat to the students of St. Edmund's College,
who were to be ordained on the Ember Saturday in September.
In November the new church at Derby, the first of Pugin's
churches of any importance, and pronounced by the High
Anglicans to be "a painfully pleasing edifice," was opened,
and the dedication sermon preached by Dr. Wiseman.

Shortly after his return to Rome, he was consulted by
Gregory XVI. as to the propriety of increasing the Bishops
in England; and on the 11th May, 1840, the propaganda
nominated four extra Vicars Apostolic, or Bishops in
partibus, Dr. Wiseman being appointed Coadjutor Bishop to
Dr. Walsh of the Midland District. His consecration took
place on Whit-Sunday at the English College, by H. E.
Cardinal Franzoni, the assistant Bishops being Dr. Kyle, V.A.
in Scotland, and Dr. Laurent, V.A. of the north of Europe.
The new Bishop's title was that of Melipotamus, the last who
had borne it having laid down his life for the faith in Cochin
China. And now came a painful parting. After a residence
in the eternal city of twenty-two years, during four Pontificates,
and having formed deep friendships with all that were good,
learned, and wise in its precincts—having lived as pupil,
Professor, Vice-Rector, and Rector in the same house—having
worthily gained the honour and esteem of all that were
honourable and estimable, the pang of parting must have been
great indeed, and much did the late Cardinal often express it
to have been.

On his arrival in England, Bishop Wiseman was at once
installed as President of St. Mary's College, Oscott, near
Birmingham. He was received with open arms by Bishop,
Professors, and Students—the latter of whom presented him
with an address, to which, in reply, the new Bishop "offered
himself to them as their fellow-labourer in the noble cause in
which they were engaged, and entreated them to allow him to
bear a part in all their burdens, and to take upon his own
shoulders the weightiest of them all."

Oscott, during Bishop Wiseman's Presidency, became
the great centre for all those whose minds tended to Catholicity. "In him the Oxford divines found first a sympathising
antagonist, and then a warm friend and ally. Many a soul

first saw there the beauty of Christian holiness; and amid the splendid functions, the solemn retreats, and the atmosphere of cheerful Catholic piety which pervaded the place, contracted a tincture of religion which almost compensated for the want of a Catholic education, and which no subsequent vicissitudes or trials will be able to efface." Bishop Wiseman's literary powers shone out with remarkable brilliancy at this period. The *Dublin Review* teemed with articles from his pen, about which it is enough to say that they silenced controversial opponents, augmented the list of converts, and blunted the shafts of Anti-Catholic literature. In conjunction with the late Saintly Father Ignatius, Bishop Wiseman issued prayers for the conversion of England, and wrote to most of the Bishops on the Continent to solicit the assistance of our foreign brethren in the faith. Their prayers were answered by inumerable conversions. During his Presidency of Oscott College, Bishop Wiseman's talents as a preacher were called into requisition at the opening of nearly all the new Catholic Churches with which the central district was more particularly being covered about this time. In 1841, in his letter on "Catholic Unity," Bishop Wiseman thus answered those who had reproached him with a too strong leaning towards the High Anglican party :—" Are we, who sit in the full light, to see our friends feeling their way towards us through the gloom that surrounds them, and faltering for want of an outstretched hand, or turning astray for want of a directing voice, and sit on and keep silent, amusing ourselves at their painful efforts, or, perhaps, allow them to hear from time to time only the suppressed laugh of one who triumphs over their distress? God forbid! If one must err, if, in the mere tribute to humanity, one must needs make a false step, one's fall will be more easy when on the side of two theological virtues, than when on the cold bare earth of human prudence. If I shall have been both too hopeful in my motives, and too charitable in my dealings, I will take my chance of smiles at my simplicity both on earth and in heaven. Those of the latter, at least, are never scornful." In 1845, Bishop Wiseman's health having suffered from too great application to literary labours, he was induced to pay a visit to the land of his birth for a few months. In 1846, Gregory XVI. expired, and was soon succeeded by Pius IX., to the great joy of the Christian world. On the 12th August, 1847, the venerated Bishop Griffiths,

Vicar-Apostolic of the London District was removed from this earth. At this time Bishop Wiseman was on his way to Rome, and two days after his arrival in that city he received a decree from the Sacred Congregation of Propaganda Fide, "appointing him Pro-Vicar Apostolic of the London District, during the goodwill and pleasure of the Holy See, with all faculties that would be enjoyed by a Vicar-Apostolic." On the following October it was reported in the public papers that "Bishop Walsh, of the Midland district, is now Archbishop of Westminster, and that Dr. Wiseman was to be Bishop of Birmingham." This information was of course premature. The fact was that Bishop Walsh was appointed Vicar-Apostolic of the London district towards the end of the autumn. During his Pro-Vicarate, Bishop Wiseman opened St. George's Cathedral, Southwark. To this ceremony this illustrious Prelate, wishing to make a grand demonstration of Catholic unity, invited many of the foreign Bishops. Some came over in answer to his appeal, and had it not been for the disturbed state of the Continent at that time (July, 1848) many others would have accepted the invitation. The opening of this vast structure, the largest built in this country since the "Reformation" (by 15 Bishops and 300 Priests) was an event of great importance, and excited the greatest attention throughout the kingdom. This was followed (in August) by the opening of Salford Cathedral, at which Bishop Wiseman also preached the dedication sermon.

On the 18th February, 1849, the venerable Bishop Walsh departed, and was in due course succeeded by Bishop Wiseman, as Vicar Apostolic of the London district. The next great point in the Cardinal's life was the one which had been so long wished, prayed, and petitioned for by the English Catholics.

On a sultry afternoon in August, 1850, a long file of carriages might have been seen proceeding from the episcopal residence in Golden Square, towards the railway station. It was Bishop Wiseman escorted by a number of his friends, who knew that he was *en route* for Rome, where the cardinalitial dignity with which he had long been invested *in the breast* of the Holy Father was now to be publicly conferred on him. The news of his elevation not only to that high dignity but to the Archiepiscopal See of Westminster—now first created for him as its primary occupant—the intelligence, in fact, that another Catholic Hierarchy was now created for England, and that an Episcopal Bench, equal in number to that of the Apostolic College now actually "governed, and would continue to govern," Catholic England, took Protestant England by surprise. Anger was expressed in many quarters, and passionate speeches were uttered, but the ferment soon subsided before the calm dignity, and conciliatory bearing, and unanswerable explanations of Cardinal Wiseman. On St. Michael's day (September 29), 1850, His Holiness Pope Pius IX. issued letters apostolic, conceived in terms of great weight and dignity, wherein he substituted for the eight Apostolic vicariates heretofore existing, one archiepiscopal or metropolitan, and twelve episcopal sees; repealing, at the same time, and annulling all dispositions and enactments made for England by the Holy See, with reference to its late form of ecclesiastical government. Bishop Wiseman was appointed on the same day by the Pope to the Archiepiscopal See of Westminster, with the administration of the Episcopal See of Southwark. On the following day, Archbishop Wiseman was raised in private consistory to the rank of Cardinal priest of the holy Roman Church, under the title of St. Pudentiana, a church in Rome, in which St. Peter is believed to have enjoyed the hospitality of the noble and partly British family, of the Senator Pudens. On the 7th October, the Pope himself invested the new Cardinal Archbishop of Westminster, with the pallium, the badge of metropolitan jurisdiction. On the same day, his Eminence issued a pastoral letter, containing these tidings from "out of the Flaminian gate of Rome;" no one but the Pope having the right to date his pastorals from the city of Rome. These documents, or rather the distortion of them, by some of the public journals, roused a complete frenzy throughout the country, which spirit was most unfairly used for political purposes, by a member of Her Majesty's government, who added fuel to the fire by the "Durham letter." In the meantime the Cardinal Archbishop of Westminster was hurrying homewards, though implored to delay by the more timid of his Eminence's advisers. It was rumoured that the government would prevent him from landing, but at length the Cardinal reached London, and at once set about discovering what all the popular frenzy was about. In one night he composed, wrote, and sent to the press his noble, manly, and unanswerable "Appeal to the reason and good feeling of the English people." Crowds besieged Mr. Richardson's London warehouse in Fleet Street to obtain copies, and a sovereign was offered for one on the eve of publication. It appeared in extenso the next morning in the columns of the *Times*, and was thus before the close of the day read by hundreds of thousands in all parts of the kingdom. On the 6th December, the feast of St. Nicholas, the Cardinal was enthroned in St. George's Cathedral, and on the following Sunday, the 8th, preached in the morning, and on the same evening began the first of three of his lectures on the "Hierarchy." The church was crowded even to the standing room, by a mixed congregation of Catholics and Protestant, and never did the Cardinal deliver any discourses with greater fervour, energy, and animation. The Cardinal spoke from a platform (erected for the mission which was going on in the church), whence his figure and action were seen to great advantage. And though, in his first lecture he said, " he would endeavour to avoid whatever might seem of a personal character," it was evident to the immense audience (the largest ever assembled in the church), that the Cardinal *felt* he was addressing, through them, the whole English nation, in defence of the simple act of a change in the internal government of the Catholic church in England, of which he took upon himself the whole responsibility. The lectures were published the day after delivery, and their circulation was enormous. During this trying period his Eminence was ever cheerful, as those who had the happiness to be near him will testify. Although he had to deplore the defection of one or two time-serving Catholics, the Cardinal must have felt amply consoled by the address of the Catholic nobility and gentry of England, who, though not claiming a share in the merit of re-constructing the Catholic Hierarchy, would not allow the Cardinal to stand alone in bearing the odium it had caused, but came forward to spread abroad their entire and cordial approbation of the measure. This address was signed by nine peers, fourteen sons of peers, twelve baronets, and several hundred untitled gentry, and members of the learned professions. But it would be unwise to continue to discant on these trying times, now that the waves of oblivion are rolling over them. It will suffice to say, that the Cardinal "fought the good fight" so well, and out-lived all its bitterness, so as to see himself esteemed and respected, if not beloved, by the noble hearted and generous English nation.

Of course the re-construction of the Hierarchy, in all its parts and constitution, entailed a large amount of application and labour, and to this work the Cardinal devoted himself. In July, 1852, was held the first Provincial Synod at St. Mary's, Oscott, before which Dr. Newman preached his beautiful Sermon "on the Second Spring" of the English Church, and at which many most important measures were concerted for the better ordering matters ecclesiastical, in this country. Diocesan Synods were also held, and conferences established in each diocese.

In 1853, the various articles which the Cardinal had contributed, from its commencement in the "*Dublin Review*," were reprinted in three volumes, and in that form attracted a great deal of attention among the Anglican party, particularly the younger portion of them. The Bishop of Amiens having obtained from Rome the relics of St. Theodosia in 1854, prepared to receive them in his Cathedral with great splendour and religious festivity. He invited several foreign prelates to attend, among others, Cardinal Wiseman. We have already alluded to the Cardinal's Sermons in Italian at the Sardinian Chapel, and on this occasion he was called upon to preach in French before the elite of the French Clergy, which he is said to have done with amazing facility. His Eminence has often preached in French at the French Chapel in London, on the occasions of the first Communion and Confirmation of the exiled Princes of France. In his introduction to the *Life of Cardinal Mezzofanti*, the learned President of Maynooth thus speaks of Cardinal Wiseman's claims to be a philologist and linguist of the first rank. "His latest writings shew, that through all the engrossing duties in which he has been engaged, he has continued to cultivate the science of philology; the Cardinal is, moreover, an accomplished linguist. Besides the ordinary learned languages, he is master not only of Hebrew and Chaldee, but also of Syriac, Arabic, Persian, and Sanscrit. In modern languages, he has few superiors. He speaks with fluency and elegance French, Italian, German, Spanish, and Portugese; and in most of these languages he has frequently preached or lectured, extempore, or with little preparation."

In 1855, the Cardinal lectured at the solicitation of the "Society of Arts," in connection with the Educational Exhibition at St. Martin's Hall, on "Home Education of the Poor."

These lectures, without any parade of learning, without any exaggeration of description for effect, but with a most accurate appreciation of the best method of dealing with the subject, are models of their class. But the large hall being used for the Exhibition, they were delivered in the smaller one, and thus deprived thousands of the gratification of hearing them. They were afterwards published by Routledge. When it was proposed to issue a number of Catholic popular tales, his Eminence highly approving the undertaking, kindly offered to contribute a work to the series—and the delightful sketch of the Church of the Catacombs—*Fabiola*, was the result, written (as the Cardinal tells us) "at all sorts of times and places, early and late, in scraps and fragments of time, when the body too fatigued, or the mind too worn out for heavier occupation; in the road side inn, in the halt of travel, in strange houses, in every variety of situation and circumstance—sometimes trying ones" —it at once took a hold on the public attention, went quickly through several editions, and is translated into every European language. In 1858, appeared his Eminence's *Recollections of the four last Popes, and of Rome in their times*, of this work, even the *Athenæum* could but speak in praise, saying that "Cardinal Wiseman has here treated a special subject with so much generality and geniality, that his recollections will excite no ill-feeling in those who are most conscientiously opposed to Papal domination."

Frequent mention has been made in the public papers of the Cardinal's composition of a drama. This was a sacred drama, in two acts, entitled the "Hidden Gem," being an episode in the romantic life of the holy St. Alexius. It is affectionately dedicated to the Right Rev. Mgr. Newsham, D.D., my tutor in boyhood, my professor in youth, and my friend through life," and was composed for the Jubilee of St. Cuthbert's College, Ushaw. This Jubilee was celebrated in July, 1858, with great splendour and much rejoicing, in the presence of the Cardinal Archbishop, Bishop Hogarth of Hexham (in whose diocese Ushaw college is situated), Bishop Briggs of Beverley, Bishop Roskell of Nottingham, Bishop Clifford of Clifton, Bishop Amherst of Northampton, Bishop Gillis of Edinburgh, and a large concourse of clergy, and old and young alumni of St. Cuthbert's, and their friends. On this memorable occasion the Cardinal presented to the College a ring which was taken off the finger of the body of St. Cuthbert in 1537. Besides the drama, the Cardinal composed a Jubilee Ode which is here given, as it, perhaps, shows more than any of his works, how, from his exalted station of Prince of the Church, and Catholic Metropolitan of England, he could condescend to write this little poem, in which he enters with all the spirit of a school boy, into the duties, tasks, joys, and games, of that happy period of life.

JUBILEE ODE.

"No breezes play, no sunbeams smile
Throughout the length of Britain's isle,
Upon a more loved honoured pile
    Than this our College home.
Heir of the rays which no more shine
In Finchal's vale, on banks of Tyne,
Round holy Cuthbert's rifled shrine,
    Or Bede's yet hallowed tomb.

CHORUS.

Then join in chorus, man and boy,
Long reign in this our noble College,
Celestial truth and earthly knowledge,
Study's toil and virtue's joy.
    (Repeated after each verse).

We love our church, its image, stalls,
Our graceful chapels, noble halls,
Our ambulacra's pictured walls,
    Our library's rich lore.
We love our ball-place, lake, and bounds,
Our merry games' perennial rounds,
The hubbub of their joyful sounds,
    Shouts, cheers, and laughter's roar.

But hush! good spirits fill the air:
They come our joy and love to share,
Great Lingard, Gibson, Gillow, Eyre,
    Who sleep beneath our sod.
And many a one whose youthful head
Soon drooped above the tainted bed,
Then sank among the martyred dead,
    The path here taught who trod.

Then up, up, cheerily, dash we on;
Not words, but deeds, mark Ushaw's son;
The world's wide battle-field upon,
    With evil and deadly strife!
In faith, uncompromising zeal,
Devotion to our country's weal,
Charity, honour, virtue—seal
    Brothers! our coming life."

In the autumn of 1858, at the invitation of the Bishop of Clonfert, his Eminence visited Ireland to preach the dedication sermon of the new church of St. Michael, Ballinasloe. From the time of his arrival to that of his departure from its hospitable shores, his journeys were as so many popular ovations. His presence was everywhere hailed with affectionate veneration and acclaim. The people and the clergy everywhere flocked round him, and everywhere he received a true Irish welcome, a real *ceadmille failthe*. In Ballinasloe he was entertained at a banquet, at which all the Prelates and the principal Clergy of the province were present. Neither were the Catholic gentry of Connaught niggard in their welcome of the illustrious Prelate. An address, signed by the High Sheriff, Pierce Joyce, Esq., spoke, in appropriate phraseology, the admiration and good wishes of the Catholics of the county of Galway. The inhabitants of Athlone also welcomed his Eminence, and gave expression to their feelings of respect in an admirable address. After this short excursion into the "Land of the West," the Cardinal Archbishop returned to Dublin. On the evening of his arrival he was the guest, at a magnificent banquet in the Mansion House, of the Lord Mayor. The following day he proceeded on a visit to Barmeath, the seat of Lord Bellew. At Dundalk he was received with joyous enthusiasm, and in the beautiful church of St. Patrick, in the presence of an immense congregation, which included a large number of clergy and eight Bishops, he delivered a sermon which was pronounced to be a masterpiece of pulpit oratory. In the evening he was present at a public-banquet which took place in the Court House, and here addresses were also presented from the clergy of Armagh and the people of the town, to each of which he replied in his accustomed felicitous manner. His Eminence then again returned to Dublin, and preached in the Cathedral on the succeeding Sunday. The next day he delivered a lecture in the Rotundo, before an immense auditory, which included the principal Catholics and many of the leading Protestants of the city. The subject of the lecture was "*The Ornamental Glass found in the Catacombs.*" During his sojourn in Dublin, he was everywhere greeted with the liveliest manifestations of affectionate respect. He was presented with addresses of welcome from all the Catholic societies. He visited and minutely examined all the public institutions. At the Catholic

University the reception was an enthusiastic ovation, joined in spontaneously by students and professors with a like zest and heartiness. The College of St. Patrick, Maynooth, was also visited, and its numerous *alumni* accorded to the Cardinal Archbishop such a reception as will long be remembered by those who had the privilege of witnessing it. The schools of the Christian brothers, Richmond Street—Ireland's great benefactors—were not omitted from the list of his visits. On the important subject that "scientific progress should assist moral improvement," he delivered a lecture before the "Young Men's Society," in the Music Hall. He then visited Carlow, Kilkenny, Waterford, and Aylward's Town, the birthplace of his mother. In each he was received with all the respect and enthusiastic rejoicing due to his great ability, his services, and the eminent position he occupied. His journey through the south was a perfect triumphal march—a joyous, spontaneous ovation, unalloyed by any annoyances or interruption. He returned to Dublin, and having preached in the Church of St. Andrew, Westland Row, left for England.

On the return of the Cardinal Archbishop to London he delivered a lecture on his "Impressions of a recent visit to Ireland," for the benefit of the Society of St. Vincent de Paul, at the Hanover Square Rooms.

In January, 1859, his Eminence visited the north of England, and at Liverpool witnessed the performance of his drama, the "*Hidden Gem*," at the Catholic Institute. He also delivered a lecture at the Philharmonic Hall on the all important subject, "*Is the education of the poor of a sufficiently practical character, or can this be imparted to it?*" In the following month his Eminence delivered a lecture at the Greenwich Institute on "*Literary Forgeries.*" In the Lent of this year the Cardinal preached a series of discourses in the Pro-Cathedral on the "Claims of Revelation and modern attacks on it." The third Provincial Synod of Westminster was held at St. Mary's College, Oscott, 12th July, 1859, at which his Eminence delivered two magnificent discourses. In the following November the Cardinal had an attack of illness, and he left England for Rome, accompanied by his physician, Dr. Munk. In the March, 1860, his Eminence sent his second pastoral letter from out the Flaminian Gate, calling upon his spiritual children to come to the temporal assistance of our Holy Father the Pope in his trouble and affliction. This magnificent pastoral being much longer than usual was divided into two portions, and read in all the Churches on two successive Sundays. His flock nobly responded to the pastor's appeal, and in the course of the summer £6,340 were remitted to the Cardinal at Rome by the Committee. And now he was anxiously expected to return, when the sad news of a relapse of his illness arrived, followed by that of a serious operation for carbuncle. Upon this his surgeon-extraordinary, Mr. Cesar Hawkins, was telegraphed for, and proceeded to attend the Cardinal at Rome. During this period the greatest anxiety and longing desire was felt by the whole diocese for news of the Cardinal's health. Telegrams arrived from Rome almost daily, and the Catholic papers were eagerly sought for, as they each week recorded the progress of his Eminence. At length his convalescence was reported, and that he had been invited by his Holiness the Pope to spend some time at his country palace at Castel Gondolfo, near Rome. The Cardinal being sufficiently recovered to perform the journey homewards, left Rome in August, and came by short stages till he reached Paris. Here his Eminence had another attack of carbuncle, and Mr. Cesar Hawkins was again sent for, and performed an operation upon the Cardinal. He at length reached London, but was ordered by his medical advisers to abstain from exertion of any kind whatever, and retire to his country seat at Low Leyton, Essex, and afterwards for a short period to Folkestone. During this convalescence the Cardinal composed the beautiful "*Hymnus in Honorem Sti. Edmundi.*" In October the Cardinal returned to town, and received congratulatory addresses from the Chapter of Westminster and other bodies on his recovery. But from this time he continued in a very precarious state of health—a state which rendered him always liable to attacks of illness, any of which might have proved serious, and which made him unequal to much active exertion, and require precautions which, under other circumstances, might have seemed unnecessary. The Cardinal again suffered from ill-health in the early part of 1861.

In June, 1861, the Cardinal Archbishop instituted the "Academia of the Catholic religion," and opened its meetings himself by an inaugural discourse. The Cardinal paid a visit to Belgium and Holland in the September following, and during the short stay of a few hours at Ostend, received an address of respect from 60 Polish gentlemen. His Eminence's health was so far re-established by this tour that he was enabled to assist, but not preach, at the Christmas festival at the Pro-Cathedral, at which time an address of congratulation on the recovery of his health was presented to him by the congregation of St. Mary's, and another on the same subject from the Chapter of Westminster.

In the spring of 1862, the Cardinal Archbishop left London for Rome to assist at the Canonization of the Martyrs of Japan, which took place with great solemnity and magnificence. On this visit to the Eternal City an event happened which proved the high opinion entertained of his Eminence by the Catholic Episcopate. At a large meeting of the Bishops of Christendom, Cardinal Wiseman was elected to preside, and afterwards to draw up the address of fervent devotion to the Spiritual and Temporal Power which was to be presented to our Holy Father the Pope. Shortly after his return to London, in July, the Chapter of Westminster presented an address to his Eminence on his sixtieth birthday; and on the 27th of the same month (August), he presided at the Annual Dinner of St. Cuthbert's Society at the Crystal Palace. In September his Eminence paid a visit in North Wales; and on his return assisted pontifically at the pro-Cathedral of St. Michael and the Angels attached to the Benedictine Monastery near Hereford, and received an address from the venerable body of English Benedictines. For years efforts had been made to obtain or erect a church for the numerous German Catholics in the eastern part of the metropolis. At length, through the exertions of the Rev. A. Purcell, an old chapel was purchased, and, after suitable alterations and decorations, was solemnly opened by the Cardinal Archbishop, assisted by the Bishop of Munster and several English Bishops. But the very precarious state of the Cardinal's health prevented him from preaching on this as on various other occasions at which he assisted pontifically. In the October of this year many public disturbances, called "Garibaldi riots," took place in various parts of the Kingdom, and at last broke out in London in Hyde Park. The Cardinal issued a pastoral in which he shewed his love for peace and order, by affectionately but firmly exhorting the Irish portion of his flock to abstain from taking any part in these disgraceful proceedings, and it is doubtless owing to this pastoral, seconded by the able exertions of the Catholic clergy in the most populous districts of London, that riots were prevented which might have ended in bloodshed.

Cardinal Wiseman's health did not admit of much exertion in the early part of 1863; however, his Eminence preached on Easter Sunday in the pro-Cathedral, was seated, and evidently suffering from the exertion. The Rev. Raphael Melia, the Italian Chaplain of the Royal Sardinian Chapel in Lincoln's Inn Fields, had in 1851 projected the erection of a church for the large body of Italians resident and constantly passing through London. Ground was purchased in Hatton Wall, Hatton Garden; but many legal and pecuniary difficulties beset his path, till at last success crowned his exertions, and those of his worthy confrére, the Rev. Dr. Faa di Bruno. The Cardinal Archbishop had always felt and taken an especial interest in this work, and it was, therefore, with great joy that, assisted by eleven English and one Scotch Bishop (Bishop Gillis, who preached the dedication sermon, and has since departed) he dedicated this vast and noble Church to the service of the Almighty on the 16th April, 1863.

A Catholic Congress having been convened to meet at Malines, to it went the great Catholic celebrities of Europe, and among them the Cardinal Archbishop of Westminster. During his stay there he was the guest of the Cardinal Archbishop of Malines. On August 18th, Cardinal Wiseman delivered before the Congress an address on the "Religious and Social position of Catholics in England." In this discourse his Eminence pourtrayed the progress of the Church in England from the time of Catholic emancipation to the present day.

The following extracts from the Cardinal's address will serve to illustrate the wonderful development of the faith since the hierarchy was re-constructed:—

"It was by a providential arrangement that the restoration of the Hierarchy took place by degrees. If it had been restored at once in 1829 we should not have been strong enough to make use of the new power thus placed at our disposal. The census of 1831 stated the population of England to be 13,000,000. In 1841 it was 15,000,000; in 1851 it rose to 17,000,000, and in 1861 to 20,000,000. During the same interval of time the number of Priests had increased in a still greater degree than the population. In 1830 there were in England 434 Priests. In the present year we have 1,242 [now 1340]. In 1830 there were 410 Catholic Churches in England; we have now 872 [941]. The number of religious houses of nuns was in 1830 only 16; it is now 162 [187]. There were for a long time no religious houses for men in England; in 1850 there were 11; we have now 55 [58].

" In London the progress of Catholicity has met with more obstacles than elsewhere. For not only is that vast capital the centre of Protestant organization, the seat of all those powerful societies which have for their avowed object the destruction of Catholicity, the residence of the Court and the nobility, and the scene of the operations of a strong press banded together against our religion, but we have also material difficulties to contend with of which many do not think. It is not in London, therefore, that Catholic Churches and Colleges are to be found, but in other dioceses, but that we are progressing even in London, the following figures will prove :—

	Churches.		Convents.		Monasteries.		Hospitals, Orphanages, &c.
1829	29	...	1	...	0	...	0
1851	46	...	9	...	2	...	4
1863	102	...	25	...	15	...	34

" I have recently opened two churches, one for Germans, and one for Italians, served by Priests of those nations, and I hope soon to be able to open a new church, where Divine service will be celebrated by French Priests, and to which a Flemish Priest will be attached." This work was on the eve of accomplishment at the Cardinal's death.

" In London, we have an hospital attended by twenty-four Sisters. A convert has founded this institution. In another diocese a convert has built a church large enough to be the diocesan Cathedral. It is served by Priests of the Benedictine Order. The churches and presbyteries in England, which have been built by converts, amount to forty-two; and in England to build a Church is to found a parish.

" You are all aware that when the Catholic Hierarchy was re-established in 1850, a violent storm of public opinion burst upon us, because of the exercise of an act of religious authority which conferred upon us no temporal power whatever. But I hasten to add that our fellow-countrymen have since that time made reparation to us so completely, that all recollection of those unhappy days is now entirely effaced from our memory. Since the re-establishment of the Hierarchy in 1850, we have held three Provincial Councils. We have Chapters to take the proper ecclesiastical steps when Bishoprics become vacant. We have also the germs of the parochial system. The Bishops have also bound themselve to endeavour to establish large Seminaries as soon as possible. All this has the Catholic Church accomplished in England by its own strength alone."

In 1839 there was not a single house of religious men in the London district, there are now 17. And one of the last acts of the Cardinal was to confirm the appointment of the Oblates of Mary Immaculate to the charge of a new mission at Kilburn. There are also thirty-one houses of religious women, of which twenty-six were introduced into the diocese under the pontificate of Cardinal Wiseman.

On his return from Belgium, his Eminence delivered a lecture at the Hartley Institution, Southampton, to inaugurate the thirty-fourth session of the Polytechnic Institution of that ancient town. The subject was "Self Culture," and the lecture lasted upwards of two hours, and was thus eulogized in the *Times*,—"Amidst the multiplicity of lectures, this lecture stands out, and has a character of its own, as obviously giving the experience of an eminent man, upon a question which touches everybody's interest and curiosity, the important question how he is to make the most of himself."

On Christmas-day his Eminence both assisted and preached at the pro-Cathedral, and made an impressive appeal on behalf of the *Providence Row Night Refuge*, established in the district by the worthy Rector, for the nightly reception of the poor who have no fixed abode, and which has now become one of the leading Catholic charities of the metropolis.

In the early part of 1864, the Cardinal became prostrated by sickness, yet he again preached with the semblance of renewed strength and health at St. Mary's, on Easter-day, and when he again lectured at the South Kensington Museum on "The Prospects of London Architecture" (a lecture highly praised in all the artistic journals), on the 17th of April, and two days afterwards delivered before the

Academy of the Catholic Religion, a discourse on " The Truth of Narratives which many persons had deemed Fabulous;" his friends began to hope that his health had become quite re-established, and to look forward to his spending many years of a life so truly valuable to the Catholic Church in England. On May 3rd, his Eminence assisted and preached at the opening of the new church of St. Mary, Turnham Green, and twelve days afterwards officiated and preached on Whit-Sunday at the pro-Cathedral.

A few years back, the Cardinal (whose love and tenderness for the poor portion of his flock was ever a great characteristic of his pastoral care), had, in conjunction with several distinguished converts, opened a house in Great Ormond Street as a Hospital for Incurables, under the patronage of St. Elizabeth of Hungary, and served by Sisters of Mercy. This house being found too limited for the purpose, the adjoining one was purchased, and was soon afterwards razed, and on its site a Convent and Church was erected by the munificence of Sir George Bowyer, Bart., M.P., and Knight of Malta. This Church, a perfect gem of Italian architecture, was opened by his Eminence on the Festival of St. John (June 24, 1864), who preached, on the occasion, from the text " Heal the Sick," a beautiful sermon on the care the Church has always shown in all ages and in all countries of its poor sick members, and gave an interesting sketch of the many grand institutions for this object in Rome and the Catholic countries of Europe. In the following month (July) his Eminence preached on the occasion of the opening of the new organ at St. Mary's, Chelsea; and at the dedication of the new church at Hanwell; and presided at a dejéuner for St. Joseph's Alms Houses (in connection with the Aged Poor Society) at the Crystal Palace.

The last religious function at which Cardinal Wiseman assisted and preached was on his fête day (St. Nicholas), 6th December, 1864. The religious ladies of " La Sainte Union" (an educational institute for young ladies) had on this day 1861, entered the Diocese of Westminster, and after having been established two years in Camden Town, had purchased two mansions on Highgate Rise, and having converted the conservatory of one into a very pretty little chapel, his Eminence promised the good nuns to be present and preach at its opening. His Eminence fixed for this purpose the third anniversary of their arrival in London, and which happened to be his own fête. The privileged few (of which the writer was one) who were invited to that beautiful function can never forget it. High mass was sung by the Rev. Abbé de Brabant, the founder of the order, in the presence of the Right Rev. the Hon. and Rev. Dr. Clifford, Bishop of Clifton (who had previously blessed the chapel and house), and a few of the London clergy who had been specially invited to assist. After the gospel, the Cardinal preached, taking for his text; "Brethren, be mindful of your prelates." His Eminence, who was then far from being well, sat on the faldstool in front of the altar, and like another St. John, spoke the last words which his flock were to hear from his lips—spoke to the tender lambs of his flock in loving and affectionate terms. It is to be regretted that no report of this sermon appeared, but we trust it may be found among the Cardinal's papers and given to the world, though this is not very likely, as his Eminence said he had prepared no set sermon, but came to speak to them familiarly of the saint whose name he had received in baptism, and to whom he had looked up to with reverence throughout his life. And he had on all occasions, which depended on himself, chosen his fête for commencing any great work (notably he had taken possession of his Diocese of Westminster on that day), and on the day on which he spoke, land for a new church and mission to be dedicated to St. Nicholas had been acquired. (This was understood to be at Twickenham.) The Cardinal then affectionately addressed the nuns and their young charge, and concluded by expressing a wish for the success of this house, and many others of the order, which were or might be established in England. After a frugal repast, his Eminence went into the guest room, and the young ladies being ranged round him, presented him with an address of respect and affection. His Eminence, in reply, spoke very kindly and encouragingly, and promised a silver medal to be worn for a month by the *best* scholar, and on the same one obtaining it three months in succession, she was to have a handsome rosary, or beautiful book. Then playfully taking the three youngest (one just six) by his side, he said he sat for a model of his patron, usually represented with three children at his feet. Never was the great Cardinal so happy as when surrounded by children. It was a great recreation for him to go and spend an afternoon in one of the convents of his diocese; give the children a holiday, and have them round him, amusing, instructing, and encouraging them.

The Cardinal a few days after this happy fête, having taken a drive to Pimlico, went on to Battersea Park. He took cold and returned to his house never to leave it alive. He had been announced to preach at the re-opening of the Church of the Rosary, Marylebone Road, but was too ill to attend. His Eminence rallied somewhat in December, and promised to assist, if not preach, at the pro-cathedral of St. Mary's on Christmas day. But as he could not leave his house, he sent the following letter, which was read from the pulpit on that day :—

"My Dear Dr. Gilbert—I had hoped to have had the consolation of giving my blessing in person to your congregation this Christmas Day, but prudential reasons, insisted upon by my medical advisers, confine me to the house. It is a disappointment to me, but I hope that this precautionary measure may enable me on subsequent festivals to impart to them that Benediction which I must ask you now to assure them I call down upon them with all my heart.

"At the same time I should wish to add my voice in favour of the Night Refuge for which the collection is made in your Church on Christmas Day. It is a charity so strictly in harmony with the devotions of this holy season, and the homeless poor whom it benefits are so precisely those who represent to us most vividly Our Blessed Lord and His holy Mother at Bethlehem, that I do not doubt that your devout congregation will largely and generously assist the good work of your Night Refuge.

" Wishing you, your Reverend Brethren, and your flock all the joys of a holy Christmas,

"I remain, my dear Dr. Gilbert,

" Yours affectionately in Christ,

"N. CARD. WISEMAN.

"8, York-place, Dec. 24th, 1864."

This is believed to be the last letter written by his Eminence.

The disease from which the Cardinal had been suffering was a local irritation of the foot, which incapacitated him from taking any active exercise, and for some time, even to leave the house. He was recovering from this, when on the 12th of January, 1865, erysipelas showed itself in his face, and three days afterwards so much depression of strength supervened, that serious fears were entertained, and on the evening of the 15th it was deemed advisable to administer the sacrament of extreme unction, which was performed by the Very

Rev. Canon Hearn, D.D. The next day his Eminence rallied considerably, and it was hoped that any apprehension of immediate danger had passed away. But his system had experienced a shock from which it never recovered. The erysipelas was followed by carbuncles, for which several severe operations were performed. During this period the doors of the Cardinal's residence were, from morning to night, besieged by crowds of anxious inquirers, the Queen Marie Amelie of France, members of her royal house, ambassadors, noblemen, clergymen, literary men, artists, of every shade of political and religious opinion, were incessant in their inquiries after the Cardinal's health. The newspapers gave daily, and some of them both morning and evening, bulletins of the Cardinal's state up to the moment of going to press. Masses and prayers, and the exposition of the blessed sacrament (that sweet devotion which the Cardinal had introduced into the diocese) were offered up in all the churches and chapels in London, and elsewhere, first for the recovery, and then, when all hope was past, for the happy death of the beloved pastor.

The Very Rev. the Vicar-General, the Very Rev. Canon Morris, and Monsignore Searle, Secretary and Almoner to his Eminence, were in constant attendance upon him, and everything that science could suggest or affection dictate was done to alleviate his condition. His medical advisers, (Dr Munk, and Messrs. Tegart and C. Hawkins) however, in accordance with the request of their illustrious patient, informed him unreservedly of the critical state of his health, and found him quite prepared for the issue, and perfectly resigned. Though rarely free from pain, and labouring under a most depressing malady, his Eminence never exhibited the slightest impatience or irritation of manner. On the contrary, the patience with which he endured the pain and irksomeness of his long illness, and bore the surgical operations which were thought necessary, his cheerful compliance with every suggestion, his uniform courtesy and gratitude for all that was done for him, is said to have made an impression on those who were around him, which time can never efface. He conversed in a calm and collected manner, not only with regard to his own dissolution, but in reference to those ecclesiastical matters in connection wtih his sacred office which had never ceased to occupy his attention. To him may well be applied the lines of the poet, referring to the death of one whose closing hours were illumined with faith, and fortified by resignation to the Divine will—

> "He taught us how to live; and oh! too high,
> The price of knowledge, taught us how to die."

On Sunday afternoon (5th February), the Canons of the Chapter of Westminster assembled by the Cardinal's request at his residence, and he made his profession of faith in their presence in the manner prescribed for a Bishop when in danger of death. After the Creed of Pope Pius IV. had been read for him, his own state of weakness preventing him from reading it for himself, before kissing the book of the Gospels, his Eminence said, "I wish to express before the Chapter that I have not, and have never had in my whole life, the very slightest doubt or hesitation of any one of the Articles of this faith; I have always endeavoured to teach it, and it is my desire to transmit it intact to my successor. *Sic me Deus adjuvet et hæc sancta Dei Evangelia.*" He then said, "I now wish to receive extreme unction at your hands as the seal of my profession of faith." The Cardinal, though anointed three weeks ago, having since rallied, considered himself to be now in a new danger. After receiving extreme unction he addressed the Chapter collectively, received each of them to the kiss of peace, and then gave them his blessing. During the following ten days the Cardinal gradually sank lower and lower, and spite of every nourishment which could be given, his Eminence calmly expired at eight o'clock on the morning of the 15th February, 1865.

The record of the last illness and death of this great Prince of the Church, has been written by the same hand that attended him with more than filial devotion, and to that the writer refers his readers. It is, however, with great satisfaction that he is enabled to give an earnest of what will therein be found from the discourse of Canon Morris, delivered at the solemn requiem at the Italian church, for the repose of the soul of our beloved Cardinal Archbishop, on the Tuesday following his decease :—

"His wonderful endurance of physical pain was the most noticeable thing to one observing the Cardinal's illness. He bore his sufferings with a heroic fortitude—so well, indeed, as to cause doubts that he suffered at all. He (Canon Morris) remembered the Cardinal telling him of a previous attack of a most dangerous and painful malady by which he was prostrated in Rome. Operation after operation was performed. At last it came to the crucial one, but he bore it without a murmur. 'Mai non senti,' said the Italian surgeons, 'he feels no pain;' so they thought from his state of quiescence under the knife. But the Cardinal suffered though he complained not. 'They little knew,' said he, when relating the incident, 'what little fear there was of the insensibility of mortification.' During these operations he held a crucifix in his hand; it was the consolation of his fatal illness also, and it was from the contemplation of that crucifix, and the reflection on the agonies of his Divine Master, who perished on it, that he borrowed his noblest fortitude. The last operation to which he was subjected was one of the most excruciating character—the cutting down the whole length of the eyelid. Previous to undergoing it, he cheerfully disposed himself to meet the worst, exclaiming, 'Well, it will be so much the less purgatory.' But these were only the external tokens of his great soul; it was in his interior virtues and graces that his wealth specially consisted. Foremost among these was his singular confidence in God. He hailed the coming of death as more than a release; he beautifully said he felt like a child going home for the holidays. How touching that exclamation: Heaven was, indeed, his home! This longing for death was frequently shown in his employment of the aspiration of the Apostle—'Concupisco dissolvi et esse cum Christo'—'I yearn to pass away and to be with Christ.' This was constantly in his mouth; and when he was remonstrated with, and asked would he not wish to live if it was God's good will, he shook his head and replied with a plaintive accent that would never be forgotten by those who heard it, 'Melior est mori et esse cum Christo'—'It is better to die and to be with Christ.' His eyes seemed constantly to be turned upon Heaven; its splendours and glories seemed to form the favourite subject of his meditation. He used to let half-murmured expressions drop now and again, as if unconsciously, that revealed the current of his thoughts. Once he said, as if continuing some long meditation on the happiness that awaited the elect, in whispered communing with himself,—'to rush through the angels into God.' The endlessness of eternity, the bliss that bathed the souls of the good—of such were his thoughts. 'I have never heard of anyone who was tired of the stars,' he was heard to exclaim with a child-like truthfulness. Such was his sublime conception of that marvellous problem of the never-ending. His thoughts were undividedly of God and for God in the most trying stages of his illness. Once when a dear relative called upon him, he, fearful of the effect the interview might have, lest it might detract him from the higher interests he had before his view, intimated his wish not to be disturbed. 'You know,' said he, 'I am to be kept altogether quiet.' During the five weeks that he lay on his bed of pain he talked but little; when he spoke it was but as if they caught a passing glimpse of what was underneath, like as of some stream pursuing a subterranean path which glittered here and there as it reached the light of day. He may have had an occasional wish to be here longer for his work's sake, but this was only exceptional; his most frequent desire was for death. His soul longed to be with Christ, but still it had to wait, and the prayer with which he consoled himself for the delay was told in the words—'O Lord, give me here my Purgatory.' He seemed to have laid out before him visibly the plan of his death. 'Let no one read to me when I am dying,' he instructed his attendants. It appeared to be his desire to pass away in silent meditation. When they sought to be more fully informed of his wishes, and said, ' What, my lord, would you not like the Litany read to you?' He replied, 'You mean the Commendation of a Dying Soul; yes, yes, I want the assistance of all the forms the Church prescribes ; I want that, and holy water, and everything—I want all that the Church prepares.' Thus, without shrinking, did he view the approach of death. He had accustomed himself to regard it, and he feared it not, and it came upon him cheerful and prepared. In the final moment, the thought came upon the beholder that the tremulous lips of the dying Prelate syllabled the sweet name of Jesus. They seemed to murmur it with their last breath. That sweet name was most dear to him; years before, in a sermon of his, which he had but recently published, producing it like a hidden treasure from a wise storehouse, he declared it was thus the Christian should expire ;" and thus died this great servant of Jesus with his Master's name upon his lips—

"BEATI MORTUI QUI IN DOMINO MORIUNTUR."

The following account of the last consolatory rites of religion over the remains of its illustrious head in this country, is compiled from the columns of the public journals, corrected from personal observation and official information :—

REQUIEM FOR THE CARDINAL ARCHBISHOP AT ST. JAMES' CHURCH, SPANISH PLACE.

On the day of His Eminence Cardinal Wiseman's decease, the following mortuary notice was drawn up and sent to the Bishops and Clergy by the Very Rev. Canon Morris :—

PIETATI · ET · CLEMENTIÆ · DIVINÆ
COMMENDA
SANCTISQUE · SACRIFICIIS · ADJUVA
ANIMAM
CHARISSIMI · IN · CHRISTO · PATRIS · NOSTRI

EMINENTISSIMI · ET · REVERENDISSIMI · DOMINI
N I C O L A I
TIT · S · PUDENTIANÆ · S · R · E · PRESB · CARD
ARCHIEPISCOPI · WESTMONASTERIENSIS
QUI · PLACIDISSIME · OBDORMIVIT · IN · DOMINO
JAMDIU · SUSPIRATO
DIE · XV · FEBRUARII · MDCCCLXV
VALE · MAGNE · PRAESUL
IN · VITA · NOBILIS
NOBILISISSIME · IN · MORTE
APUD · DEUM · MEMENTO · NOSTRI
ET · ECCLESIÆ · VIDUATÆ · SPONSÆ · TUÆ.

———

COMMEND
TO THE DIVINE GOODNESS AND MERCY,
AND HELP WITH THE HOLY SACRIFICE,
THE SOUL
OF OUR DEARLY BELOVED FATHER IN CHRIST,
NICHOLAS CARDINAL WISEMAN,
WHO, IN SWEET PEACE, YIELDED UP HIS LIFE,
TO
HIS DEAR LORD,
FEBRUARY XV., MDCCCLXV.,
AGED LXII. YEARS.
FAREWELL GREAT PRELATE,
NOBLE IN LIFE,
MOST NOBLE IN DEATH,
IN YOUR HOME WITH GOD,
PRAY FOR US
AND YOUR SORROWING SPOUSE
THE CHURCH.
FAREWELL!

On the following morning a solemn Requiem Mass was sung for the repose of the soul of the Cardinal Archbishop, at St. James' Church, Spanish Place (the mission in which His Eminence's town residence was situated), by the Very Rev. Canon Morris—the Rev. Alfred White being Deacon, and the Rev. E. Tunstall, Sub-Deacon. A very large number of the secular and regular clergy of the Arch-Diocese assisted at and sung the Plain Chant Requiem. On the following Tuesday a solemn Requiem was sung at the Church of the Jesuit Fathers, Farm Street, for the same intention, at which the magnificent Requiem of Mozart was performed. During the week solemn Requiem Masses were also sung or said in every church or chapel throughout the Arch-Diocese of Westminster for the repose of the Cardinal's soul, at which large crowds attended to shew their respect and love for their deceased Archbishop, and to implore the Almighty to give him speedy entry into the Divine presence.

At High Mass on the Sunday following the Cardinal's decease, his panegyric was pronounced from every pulpit amid the sobs and tears of the poor whom he had so loved, and for whom he had always shown such a tender sympathy.

THE LYING IN STATE.

The body of His Eminence the late Cardinal Archbishop of Westminster, lay in state during Friday and Saturday, in the drawing-room of his residence in York Place; and thither on those days, thousands flocked to look once more on the well-beloved face of their late Pastor, and to offer a prayer for the repose of his soul. At the entrance to the apartment was a vestibule, in which was a large carved representation of Our Saviour on the Cross. In the centre of the principal chamber, resting on a bier, was the coffin containing the remains of the deceased, attired in the Pontifical vestments of a violet colour. The Alb was one worked by the Orphans of Norwood, and bore the inscription, "Father of the Orphans, pray for them." The hands were crossed on the breast grasping a crucifix, whilst on his fingers, outside his gloves, the backs of which were embroidered in gold with the glory and "I.H.S.," were the jewelled rings which are symbolical of his being wedded to the Church. The deceased Cardinal had on his head the small scarlet cap which the Pope and Cardinals wear on ordinary but not on state occasions. At the head of the coffin, however, which was lined with white and yellow satin, was an exceedingly large and richly embroidered mitre in figured white satin, whilst at the foot were an elaborately ornamented crucifix, crozier, and other emblems of ecclesiastical dignity. On one side of the apartment, in its darkest recess, there had been erected an altar, at which were constantly kneeling and praying a number of nuns, who occasionally relieved each other, and who in their turn visited and touched the cheek and kissed the hand or the crucifix which it held in its rigid fingers. With regard to the appearance of the Cardinal in death, those who had known him in life could scarcely believe they were looking upon the remains of a man of so much bulk, and generally speaking of so robust an appearance, as he had up to his last illness exhibited. Even the body itself seemed to be much reduced, whilst the full features of the face had apparently dwindled away, denoting a large amount of prostration, and of long and extreme suffering. The coffin, consisting of an inner lead shell, and an outer one of polished English oak, was lined with gold coloured silk; the ornaments were richly gilt, and the plate on which the full arms were emblazoned (by Moring, of Holborn), bore the following inscription:—

EMUS ET RMUS DOMINUS
NICOLAUS,
TIT. S. PUDENTIANÆ S. R. E. PRESB. CARD.
WISEMAN.
PRIMUS ARCHIEPISCOPUS WESTMONASTERIENSIS
NATUS DIE 2 AUGUSTI, 1802,
CONSECRATUS DIE 8 JUNII, 1840
OBIIT DIE 15 FEBRUARII, 1865.
ORATE PRO EO.

———

THE MOST EMINENT AND REVEREND,
NICHOLAS WISEMAN,
CARDINAL PRIEST OF THE HOLY ROMAN CHURCH,
FIRST ARCHBISHOP OF WESTMINSTER;
BORN 2 AUGUST, 1802; CONSECRATED 8 JUNE, 1840;
DECEASED 15 FEBRUARY, 1865. PRAY FOR HIM.

In consequence of the crowds who pressed to see the remains of his Eminence whilst lying in state, the executors were obliged to order that none but particular friends should be admitted after Saturday. The body, however, remained in York Place until late on the following Tuesday evening, during which day a most touching service was celebrated, the Divine Office being chanted every hour by the different Religious Orders of the diocese.

One o'clock—Vespers by Carmelites and Dominicans.

Two o'clock—First Nocturn by Servites, Augustinians, Passionists, and Pius Society of Missions.

Three o'clock—Second Nocturn by Oblates of St. Mary and Marist Fathers.

Four o'clock—Third Nocturn, by Oblates of St. Charles and Fathers of Charity.

Five o'clock—Lauds, by Oratorian Fathers.

According to the usual Roman use, the Fathers of the Society of Jesus, whose institute exempts them from all choral offices, were not invited to take part in the singing of the Office. At the close of each Office, the Absolution was given by the Superior of each Order present, vested in a cope.

REMOVAL OF THE CARDINAL'S REMAINS TO THE PRO-CATHEDRAL.

On Tuesday evening, very quietly, and with total absence of ceremonial observances, the body of the Cardinal was removed from the house he had lately inhabited, in York Place, to the Pro-Cathedral of St. Mary, in Moorfields, where it rested until the funeral. A crowd, principally composed of the humbler class of Catholics, had gathered before the door as early as three o'clock in the afternoon, expecting that the removal of the corpse would take place some time that evening, and perhaps early. It was nearly half-past eleven, however, before the plain hearse, drawn by four horses, moved from the door, and midnight had struck when the sad burden was deposited in the body of the church. Encased in a leaden coffin, the remains of the lamented cardinal—lamented sincerely and affectionately, we may say, by the poor mourners, who stood in the cold rain near his doorstep, and who spoke in low voices and with tears upon their cheeks— was at last borne forth. On reaching St. Mary's, the sacred remains were received by the Rev. Clergy, and placed on the catafalque erected in the centre of the church. Early on Wednesday, masses were said at the high altar, and in the evening, at half-past six o'clock, the solemn matins and lauds were presided over by the Right Rev. Bishop Grant, of Southwark, when the church was occupied by a crowded multitude.

Words are inadequate to describe the scene which presented itself on Wednesday morning in front of St. Mary's, Moorfields, and around Finsbury Circus, when the church was opened for the public. It was a scene singularly illustrative of the vast amount of Catholic feeling and sterling devotion which is yet to be found in the very heart of this great, wealthy, worldly city—such a spectacle as, in its peculiar character, no other solemn event than the death of a great priest of the Catholic Church could have evoked. The remains of the Cardinal were laid out in solemn state in the pro-Cathedral over night; and at nine o'clock on Wednesday morning the church was thrown open to the public. But the crowds who had gathered round the sacred edifice were such that no ordinary management could attempt to cope with them without producing irremediable confusion, and perhaps danger of life or limb. In front of the pro-Cathedral, Liverpool Street was blocked up by a crowd, expectant yet orderly. A similar concourse filled up the whole of East Street, which runs along the side of the church and the Presbytery, and leads into Finsbury Circus. But the Circus itself, perhaps, presented the most singular picture. At each side, curving away from the door of the Priest's house, vast numbers of men and women were drawn up, two and three abreast, all silent and expectant, all waiting their turn of admission into the church. Their consciousness of the solemn and sorrowful character of the occasion was evinced by their orderly arrangement, and their grave and reverent demeanour. It was curious to note that concourse, so large and yet so decorous—curious to listen to their subdued speech, where none spoke, it might be said, above their breath. On the great bulk of the faces there could be perceived a marked expression of grief, as if each person had lost some near relative or dear friend.

The pro-Cathedral does not afford facilities for the admission of large crowds of persons without danger—an unavoidable result of its peculiar position, crushed into the corner of two narrow streets. But the arrangements lovingly made for the rapid admission and exit of the people, under the direction of the Rev. Dr. Gilbert, were admirable. A large force of police were drawn up under the pathway from Finsbury Circus to the narrow side entrance into the aisle. These officers formed a sort of cordon, or barrier, inside which the visitors to the church could pass only two abreast. The excellence of this arrangement will be borne in mind when it is remembered how great was the crowd and how narrow the doorway; and the manner in which the City Police acquitted themselves of this troublesome duty, their good temper, patience, and their courtesy, are deserving of all praise. Inside, a number of gentlemen, lay members of the Confraternities connected with St. Mary's, Moorfields, controlled all the arrangements. They conducted the people in regular order through the church, and out by the front gate; and, in this manner, everything approaching to confusion or irreverent crush or hurrying, was happily avoided.

A catafalque had been erected in the centre of the church, in front of the High Altar; and on this the coffin, containing the mortal remains of the great Cardinal, rested. The catafalque was draped in black, bordered and fringed with gold mourning colours corresponding to the rank of the deceased Prince of the Church. The coffin was covered with a black pall, also bordered with gold. On the head of the coffin was a cushion, also of black and gold, and on this lay the red hat with long pendant tassel, the emblem of the Cardinal's rank. From the coffin hung down, to the foot of the catafalque, a robe of blue satin, covered with stars in gold, and a similar robe of scarlet, indicative of the Sacred Orders to which the deceased Cardinal belonged. Nearly a hundred wax lights, varying in size from that of the large Paschal candle to the altar taper, burned round the catafalque, at each corner of which (nearest to the high altar) stood a member of one of the pious Confraternities in the robe and alb of his Order.

The high altar was draped in black, and all the seats ranged through the chancel for the officiating clergy were covered with black bordered with gold. The Cathedra, or archiepiscopal throne, on the left side of the high altar, was similarly draped in mourning hues. The Chapel of the Sacred Heart was likewise hung in black and gold, and railed off for the accommodation of the foreign ambassadors and their suites, who had signified their intention of being present at the solemn Offices of the Dead on Thursday morning. The Chapel of the Holy Family, on the right side of the church, was also draped in black, and set apart for other distinguished persons attending the sacred ceremonies. The rows of tall pillars dividing the aisles from the nave were covered, from capital to base, with black cloth lined around with waving gold bands. The pulpit and the stairs approaching to it were similarly draped in black, bordered with gold and covered with golden stars. In like manner was the gallery under the organ-loft covered with black starred with gold, and black curtains shrouded the windows, the monumental tablets on the walls, and the pictures of the Stations of the Cross around the sacred edifice.

The vast altar-piece which crowns the chancel—in which the awful story of a crucified God is figured by the artist's vivid imagination—was, with all its striking and impressive details, left exposed; and whilst the rest of the church, except where the hundred lights blazed round the coffin of the dead, was shrouded in solemn obscurity, as if enveloped in one great mourning shroud, the pale wintry sun streamed down through the lantern window on the vast picture which covers the whole of the chancel wall, casting its rays on the Divine central figure, on the hopeful face of the penitent thief, on the weeping Mother and her companions, on the horseman with his lance raised at that sacred side, on the trembling multitude, and on the fierce Roman soldiers who heedlessly throw the dice for possession of the seamless robe. The scene was deeply solemn, and more solemn still because of that silent living flood that unceasingly streamed in and out of the church.

Two by two the people entered, rich and poor alike. Two by two they moved round the catafalque. Silently and reverently, many with murmuring prayer—some, who, perhaps, had received kindly ministration from the consecrated hand that would be lifted, on earth at least, on their behalf no more—with smothered sob and tearful cheek. As they moved round, they were told off down the nave, and departed by the central gate. But not a few, chiefly women, stepped aside and knelt awhile to offer a heart-felt prayer to Heaven. The spectacle was a touching one; and not the least interesting part of it was the conduct of the Protestant visitors, of whom there were many. It is possible that mere curiosity may have brought many of them there; but in their demeanour in the church they exhibited none of the levity of idle curiosity. What they expected to see we cannot tell; but, assuredly, when they beheld that sacred temple draped in all the sombre and solemn panoply of mourning for the noble Priest and marvellously gifted Prince of God's Church whose remains reposed under the sable pall before them, thoughts anything but irreverent must have taken possession of their minds. Everything in the church was fitting to the solemn occasion; and so everything impressed these respectable Protestant visitors. They bowed their heads reverently, they looked round with a reverent curiosity, and silently and decorously took their departure.

Of the Catholics who crowded to take this last farewell of the great and noble Priest, Prelate, and Prince, we need not say much. They exhibited all that piety and devotion we might have looked for; and it was touching to see the anxiety of many of them to have their Rosaries or their prayer-books laid for a moment in contact with the coffin—that they might carry away, as it were, some faint afflatus of the spirit of the holy Priest whose corpse was enshrined in that last home of the dead. But so they came and so they passed away. Tears were shed and prayers were murmured; and the mighty throng who passed through the church seemed to think that, in every murmured prayer, they were rather asking blessings for themselves than for the soul of the noble Prelate, the gifted scholar, the gallant soldier of Christ, which had passed away so soon to its divine reward.

THE SOLEMN REQUIEM MASS AT ST. MARY'S.

On Thursday morning, a vast crowd had already assembled before and around the pro-Cathedral. It had been announced that the solemn Mass of Requiem would commence at 10 o'clock. But more than an hour before that time the doors were already assailed by applicants for admission. It had been arranged, in consequence of the comparatively limited accommodation which the church at Moorfields affords, that none should be admitted except by tickets previously procured; and on Wednesday there was not a ticket procurable for any available corner of the church.

Before nine o'clock on Thursday morning, the approach of carriages began; and at half-past nine, the whole building was nearly filled. Still more came and more; and the Rev. Dr. Gilbert, the Missionary Rector of Moorfields, under whose control all the arrangements lay, taxed his ingenuity to find room for the vast numbers who crowded to the doors. The Chapel of the Sacred Heart, which bordered on the principal entrance, was speedily filled by members of the foreign embassies and other distinguished personages; and in the Chapel of the Holy Family, every seat was occupied long before ten o'clock by the representatives of the noblest Catholic families in England. The rest of the church was equally crowded; and though the solemn ceremonies did not commence before a quarter to eleven o'clock, there was not at ten o'clock a single seat unoccupied.

We have already described where the catafalque and coffin lay in the centre of the nave before the high altar. This morning the dark pall had been removed, and the coffin was covered by a pall of yellow satin deeply bordered with black and fringed with gold. On the black border was a Maltese cross in white silk, and on this was the escutcheon of the late Cardinal in black, surmounted by the Cardinal's hat in crimson silk, with the impressive motto, "OMNIA PRO CHRISTO." Similar Maltese crosses, with the escutcheon embroidered in the same manner, and bordered with gold, had been placed on the dark mourning drapery in several other parts of the church.

The number of Protestant noblemen and gentlemen present was very numerous, but it was perfectly impossible, so densely crowded was the sacred building, to obtain the names of all. In front of the high altar, close to the catafalque, we noticed the Duke and Duchess of Sutherland seated beside Lord Campden. In the aisle and the Chapel of the Holy Family, there were also the Earl of Courtenay, Earl Malmesbury, the Earl and Countess of Kenmare, the Duchess of Leeds, the Marchioness of Londonderry, the Earl of Orford, the Earl of Buchan, Lord Petre, Lord Trimleston, Lord Stourton, Lord Clifford, Lord Campbell, Lord Edward Howard, Viscount Fielding, Lord Castlerosse, Lady Fitzgerald, Lord Henry Gordon Lennox, M.P., Lord Southwell, Lord Stafford, the Count Torre Diaz, Count Eyre, the Marchioness of Lothian, Lord Herries, Lord Lovat, the Dowager Countess of Buchan, Lord Arundell, Sir George Bowyer, Bart, M.P., Sir Coleman O'Loughlin, Bart.. M.P., the Hon. Mrs. Herbert, Sir Paul Molesworth, Bart., the Hon. Montague Mostyn, the Hon. Mrs. Stonor, the Right Honourable Thomas O'Hagan, the Hon. Mrs. Agar Ellis,

Mr. Justice Shee, Mr. Robert and Lady Catherine Berkeley, John A. Blake, Esq., M.P., Lady Milford, Charles Eyre, Esq., Hon. Miss Calthorpe, Chevalier de Zulueta, John Pope Hennessy, Esq., M.P., Miles O'Reilly, Esq., M.P., Sir Hungerford Pollen, Bart., &c.

Representatives of the French, Austrian, Spanish, Bavarian, Portugese, Haytian, Greek, and other embassies were also present; and the Count de Chavannes specially attended as the representative of Queen Amelie, relict of the late King, Louis Phillippe of France.

The High Mass, as we have said, began shortly before eleven o'clock. The celebrant prelate was the Right Rev. Dr. Morris, Bishop of Troy; assisted by the Very Rev. Dr. Russell, President of St. Patrick's College, Maynooth. The Deacon was the Rev. Dr. Pius Melia, the Cardinal's late Confessor, and the Sub-deacon was the Rev. Thomas Gloag, of the Order of Oratorians. The Prelates present were the Right Rev. Dr. Brown, Bishop of Newport; Right Rev. Dr. Ullathorne, Bishop of Birmingham, Right Rev. Dr. Brown, Bishop of Shrewsbury, Right Rev. Dr. Turner, Bishop of Salford, Right Rev. Dr. Grant, Bishop of Southwark, Right Rev. Dr. Roskell, Bishop of Nottingham, Right Rev. Dr. Goss, Bishop of Liverpool, Right Rev. Dr. Vaughan, Bishop of Plymouth, Right Rev. Dr. Clifford, Bishop of Clifton, Right Rev. Dr. Amherst, Bishop of Northampton, Right Rev. Dr. Cornthwaite, Bishop of Beverley, Right Rev. Dr. O'Regan, Bishop of Dora, &c.

The Prelates clad in purple copes with white mitres, occupied the sanctuary at each side of the altar; and the Provost and Canons were seated in their stalls in the choir. The choir itself and the portion of the nave and the catafalque was filled by three hundred clergymen in cassock and surplice, whose united voices, in singing the sublime Gregorian requiem, produced a most solemn and impressive effect.

A Requiem Pontifical Mass is, as our readers well know, one of the most solemn and impressive services of the Church. Unlike other ordinary Masses it lacks the magnificent music of the *Gloria* and *Credo,* nor has it even those exquisitely touching lamentations with which we are familiar as forming part of the beautiful service of *Tenebræ* in Holy Week. Nevertheless a Requiem Mass is one of the grandest services of the Church, and abounds in chants and hymns of such deep solemn pathos in their music, of such a mournful melody of woe as no description can convey to those who have not heard those last great offices of religion that Catholics pay to their most illustrious dead. The first of these sad choral efforts yesterday was the Gregorian Chant of the " Kyrie Eleison." This was delivered alternately in solo and chorus by the whole choir with an effect that was really wonderful. The most breathless silence was observed as the long wailing cadence of the chant died softly away in a kind of moan that none could listen to unmoved. After this magnificent funeral chant the Collect and Epistle were recited, the thin, weak voice of Bishop Morris coming in with most touching effect after the full, swelling sounds of the choir. The magnificent chorale of the *Dies Iræ*, this great song of fear and entreaty was given as it has certainly never been given before in England, and there was a positive murmur among the congregation as its long sad wailing chorus closed at last in intervals of melancholy sound. After this portion of the ceremony an extraordinary effect was produced by all the great choir of priests and dignitaries bearing lighted candles. The effect of this sudden illumination, which showed distinctly the features and rich dresses of the whole throng of ecclesiastics, who rose in reverence to the Gospel, was one of the most singular and impressive features of the whole ceremony.

But when the tinkle of the bell was heard, and the celebrant held aloft the consecrated host, and every Catholic knee was bent, and every Catholic head was bowed, there was not a standing figure in the whole church, except that of the aged Prelate who stood before the altar. Every Protestant present, from duke to commoner, was touched by the awful beauty of that holy sacrifice and bent his knee, and bowed his head in reverent acknowledgment.

THE FUNERAL ORATION.

At the close of the High Mass, the Right Rev. Dr. Manning, Provost of the Cathedral, ascended the pulpit and proceeded to deliver the beautiful and touching discourse of which we have his kind permission to give the following outline. It occupied about an hour in the delivery; the congregation listened with deep and rapt attention; and at more than one passage many were moved to tears. When the Right Rev. gentleman alluded to the early life of the great Cardinal, and the prophetic feeling by which his heart was moved that he should yet share in the conversion of England to the true and olden faith, none listened unmoved; but when he, with eloquent simplicity, described the last hours of the great Priest and Prince of the Church, his sufferings, his agony, and his patience and sweetness of temper through it all, there was not a dry eye in the church. Dr. Manning delivered his text as follows:—

Ecclus. xlix. 15.—" Let him be a long time remembered, who raised up for us our walls that were cast down, and set up the gates and the bars; who rebuilt our houses."

" If the command of authority had not bid me speak to-day, I should not have ventured on this task. It would be a hard task to any one. It is a harder task to me. It is beyond the power of any of us to speak as we ought of the great Pastor and Prince of the Church, who lies here in the midst of us. It is altogether beyond mine. I have, moreover, a further hindrance. The private sorrow for the loss of the kindest of friends, the last in this kind I can ever have in life.

" But as he, in his last days, unknown to me, and when I was afar off, laid on me this command, I fulfil it as I can. It is the last obedience I can render to him, whom it has been my happiness and my honour for these thirteen years very feebly but faithfully to serve.

" It would not, however, become me on such a day of public mourning to speak of any private sorrow. For to whom is not this a private sorrow and a personal grief?

" I see before me the Bishops of the Catholic Church in England shorn of their chief glory. The light which went before them is gone out, and the strong arm which struck for them is still in death. And yet it is not only a public but a private grief to you. On most of you that hand impressed the Episcopal character. He was guide, teacher, and friend to many of you, who around him grew up as his disciples and his sons.

" Of the Priesthood gathered here, perhaps the greater number either in Rome or in Oscott have learned from his lips, have been upheld and guided by his voice. The hands of many were anointed by him with unction of the Holy Sacrifice. Many perhaps would never have held out in the dangers which beset their vocation, but for his encouraging voice and his sustaining hand. You, too, have lost not only a Pastor, but a father and friend.

" Many here are his spiritual children in the Gospel of Jesus Christ. They would never have known the perfect truth as it is in Jesus but for him. Many would never have been penitents, many never Christians, but for the voice of the Good Shepherd which spoke by his lips. Many of you loved him as the kindest and tenderest of friends. Many as a benefactor, a counsellor, a comforter. To all of us, then, it is a private sorrow. And yet it rises into something more than a personal grief. There is a mourning to-day throughout the Catholic Church in England. The Pastor who has led the whole flock in the last fifteen years has gone before us, and left us in the wilderness. The solemn requiem is ascending throughout England for the repose of that great soul.

" Not in England alone, but wheresoever the English speech is known, the name of Nicholas Wiseman, the first Archbishop of Westminster, is a title of honour cherished and revered.

" And not only where our tongue is spoken, but in all languages within the unity of the Universal Church, the name and fame of our beloved and lamented Pastor is in veneration.

" The other day, when he recalled me to his side, everywhere as I travelled homewards, the first question was of that precious life. They only knew that I was an Englishman, but their first enquiry, full of sympathy and of condolence, was of his state.

" But most of all, where he was best known and most cherished, in Rome, among the friends of his youth, now princes in the Sacred College, his life was counted as of great price, and his death as the extinction of one of the brightest lights which surround the Holy See. When the Sovereign Pontiff knew that hope was all but gone, he lifted his hands and eyes to heaven, and said—' This and the loss of the Archbishop of Cologne are two heavy blows to me. The Archbishop for Prussia and the Cardinal for England at this moment were of inestimable worth. But the will of the Lord be done.'

" Our private griefs, then, lose themselves and are ennobled in this universal mourning. There will be a world-wide sorrow wheresoever the Catholic name is spread. We are all poorer by this loss, and the voice which has taught, cheered, elevated and strengthened tens of thousands in every land will be heard no more on earth. Henceforth it is mingled with the voices which are eternal.

" What, then, can I say? You know all, you feel all that can be spoken. I cannot narrate a biography the outlines and dates of which have been in these last days in all our hands.

" I cannot undertake a criticism of his wonderful gifts and powers, and of the rich fertility of the mind which will fascinate us no more. It would be a cold and heartless task.

" Least of all can I pronounce a panegyric. His name is a panegyric. The life which is before you in all its completeness, its unity, its expanding powers, its multiplying honours, its exuberant works, its calm, tranquil sunset, all this which you know already, sets before you a noble and stately picture of a great Christian, a chief Pastor of his Flock, a Prince over the Church of God.

" What, then, is left to me?

" I can but draw most faintly and most hastily the outlines of a great life. Here and there I may put in a few personal features, single touches of the beautiful colours which played about him. And a few words from that voice which, though we shall hear no more, yet speaks by the accents of the past hanging in the air, or inscribed deeply in works which cannot pass away.

" It was but the other day we were preparing to welcome as a Festival the twenty-fifth anniversary of his Episcopal consecration. The tenacity to life with which he held on through mortal sickness and ever-returning dangers had misled us into a sanguine expectation that the twenty-five years would run their course. But we shall celebrate it otherwise now. The act of to-day is, as it were, the Vigil of that Festival which we may keep still, but with other thoughts and with other records of his great career. For a great period it was. From 1840 to 1865 is perhaps the most pregnant and vivid period in the Catholic history of modern England since its great separation from Unity. I am well aware that in those five and twenty years many devout Catholics, priests and bishops, of whom some are here to-day, laboured powerfully in the work of building up in England the ruins of the Catholic order. I bear this always in mind when I speak of the career of the Cardinal Archbishop. They were around him and at his side; some were in the field before him, many have done great and notable works, some had their hands upon the very same works which are identified with him. Nevertheless, they will bear a glad and generous witness to my words, when I say that he towers above them all. The works of which I shall speak were not exclusively his. No; because the works of the Church are in common. It has one heart, one will, one strength, one arm. And yet though not exclusively his, they are emphatically his; that is, the will and providence of God used him as its instrument with special and distinguishing prominence.

" It was in the year 1863 that the Sovereign Pontiff, speaking of the Cardinal, described him as 'the man of divine providence for England.' The words struck me as visibly true and exact. But I do not know that until now I have ever seen their full exactness. We have his life now before us from its rising to its setting. We can trace it in all its times, in its period of preparation, its period of active power, its period of withdrawal from the field; and there seems to be a singular completeness about it, and a visible correspondence to the times and the country for which he laboured.

" His mission was to England in the nineteenth century, and to the most critical period of that century for us.

" The Church in England had already endured its 300 years of desolation.

" The time of the liberation of the Church had come. Catholics were free once more. The Holy Sacrifice was restored with public manifestations upon the altar.

" The emancipation was not the beginning of a movement, but itself an effect of causes long in action afar off and in other lands. The great oscillation to and from the Catholic unity which restored so much of the Catholic inheritance in foreign countries, began to work upon England. The horrors and impieties of the first French Revolution had produced a reaction towards Catholic faith and Catholic piety. The tide had turned upon the continent, and its undulations reached our shores. When the tide turns the tidal rivers rise. England began to feel the weight and the pressure of a broader and nobler religious spirit than was to be found in the 300 years of its past history. The change of our polity in 1829, let loose a flood upon this country. It had been ice-bound for generations; but the thaw had set in. After the frost came the flow, and as in the floods which inundate the land, all things are lifted, the fruits of the earth, the trees of the forest, the dwellings of men, so it was in England, when the old traditions of 300 years gave way before the larger spirit of modern legislation.

"Still more under the surface there was a movement as of many contending currents, intellectual and spiritual, hardly known while as yet the old exclusiveness held its activity in check. These vigorous and vehement movements went on year after year, multiplying in speed and volume. A crisis was come. Doubt, uncertainty, restlessness, great discontent, great licence of opinion, a craving after truth, unity, and peace, and an earnest seeking for it at all costs; absolute mistrust of the guidance and teachings of men; all this from 1830 to 1840 had been preparing a crisis in the religious life of England. 'There was no Balm in Gilead, no Physician there.' Multitudes of thoughtful and earnest men were seeking for some Mind, some Voice, some Guide, some Teacher to lead them in the way of truth and life.

"As the crisis had been preparing for him, so he had been prepared to meet it."

The right reverend preacher then commenced a brief outline of the Cardinal's early life, and of his long preparation in the centre of christendom for the great work he was destined to perform, and the great battle of the faith he was to fight in this country. He then quoted the passage from the Cardinal's "noble-hearted letter on Catholic Unity," which has been given in one of the previous pages of this work, and continued on the same subject: "In these last days I have read again and again such words as these:—'Great beginnings doomed to a great disappointment. Lofty undertakings, and it must be confessed closed by a signal failure.' Not so fast, men of this world. Not so lordly and confident, wise and prudent of the earth. The ploughing of December may be drenched with the rains of January, and the February snows hide all things from the eyes of men. But the sweat of the ploughman and of the sower is not in vain; there is a life in the sod, a stature, a symmetry, an expansion, and a maturity deep down, out of sight, coiled together, and yet unfolding in silence. There must come yet binding frosts, and scourging hail, and raving winds, but the summer's sun and the autumn fruits are sure as the march of time, and changes of day and night. You have it in an old book—not much read, it may be, in these days of light—

"'As the rain and the snow come down from heaven and return no more, but soak the earth and water it, and make it to spring and to give seed to the sower and bread to the eater, so shall my word be which shall go forth from my mouth; it shall not return to me void, but it shall do whatsoever I please, and shall prosper in the things for which I send it.' (Is. lv. 10.)

"And again: 'The husbandman waiteth for the precious fruit of the earth, patiently bearing till he receive the early and the latter rain. Be ye therefore also patient, and strengthen your heart, for the coming of the Lord is at hand.' (St. James v. 7, 8.)

"The conversion of England! Do men think that we expect the twenty millions of Englishmen to lie down Protestants at night and to wake up Catholics in the morning? Do they so little know the calm wisdom of the illustrious dead who lies here, the centre of our veneration and of our love, as to think that he was such a dreamer of day dreams, so unreal and fantastic in his hopes. He was a believer like him who for a hundred and twenty years built the ark; and a hoper like him who all alone entered imperial Rome a simple fisherman, but the Vicar of the Son of God.

"Such were his expectations; and when he closed his eyes upon England, he had already seen the work he had begun expanding everywhere, and the traditions of 300 years everywhere dissolving before it. Time is not with the church of God. Converging lines may stretch beyond our sight, and overpass the horizon, but they must intersect at last. So with the work of grace upon the country of our birth and of our love. Its desolations are not for ever."

Mgr. Manning then proceeded to dilate on the characteristics of the great Cardinal, his tenderness for the sick and poor, his forbearance of others, the generosity of his heart, his patient endurance, and finally concluded with the following sketch of his last moments:—

"The same has been conspicuous through this last season of death. But it is not in place that I should dwell upon these things now. Six weeks ago I left him restored from the suffering which we thought was transient. When we parted he was standing at the threshold of his room in the full height of his stature, as if once more in health. And, with his benediction and embrace, he dismissed me—to see him, I may say, no more. What passed in the month which followed, you already know, or in a more fitting way will know hereafter. We had so long watched him, and so long become familiar with his dangers and his recoveries, so long seen his wonderful tenacity of life, that no one was alarmed as soon as a stranger might have been. The end came at last: long looked for: and yet sudden still. He commanded me to return to him with all speed; and I came in time to receive a gaze of recognition and his blessing, and to bear to him on my knees the Benediction of the Vicar of our Lord. What I add is the record of those who had the happiness of tending him by night and day. Through the whole of that season his mind was calm, peaceful, thoughtful of others, grateful for every service, vividly alive to every intention of kindness in those about him. Once when very ill and unable to rest in any posture, one who stood by said, 'I fear you suffer much.' He answered, 'I do not suffer at all. It would be very wrong and ungrateful in me to complain, or to call a little discomfort suffering. Think of poor people. I have a good bed, and everything possible done for me.' At another time he said, 'I have made it a rule for many years never to call anything pain till it is unendurable.'

Once when an attendant endeavoured to move him so that he should not lie on the wound which the surgeon had made, he smiled and said, 'It is sore enough always, and makes very little difference in the pain.' He was always trying to save trouble to those about him, and always showed pleasure in everything that was performed for him; always saying how kind they were, and how well everything was done, just tasting and then refusing it when nature could endure no more. At one time it was necessary to give both medicines and food after midnight, while as yet it was not thought necessary or advisable to give Holy Communion by way of viaticum. This he felt most of all. He would say, 'They little know of what they are depriving me. A little fasting would tire me less than this longing.' And at another time, 'O, how much longer am I to have patience? How long am I to wait? They are keeping me from my only consolation.' When the last days of unconsciousness began, and he was hardly able to swallow for pain, as soon as he heard the words 'It is right to do this,' and 'You ought to take this,' he at once obeyed. He had put himself simply under obedience to those about him as a submission to the will of God. When told that he must undergo another operation, he at first said 'I think I cannot.' Then in a moment he said, 'No, that will not do. If it is right let it be done.' When told that if the most dangerous of the operations were not performed, he would not live till night, he afterwards playfully said, 'How unkind of them. They told me that I should have been in heaven to-night, and they have kept me out of it.' One day he was overheard to say as he was inwardly dwelling on his own great sufferings, and on the greater sufferings of One who was his Master and his model in patience, 'He showed no mercy to himself.' When his physicians finally told him that hope was gone, he thanked them with gratitude, and from that moment made his last disposition of all earthly things, and then entered into the sanctuary of God's presence, from which he never again came forth.

"To one who was always at his side, it seemed as if he were always praying, wrapt in the thought of God. Though still among men, the words of the apostle were emphatically fulfilled in him. He was dead and his life was hid with Christ in God. He had ceased to speak or to hold fellowship with us, but a greater life had expanded itself in union with the Father of Spirits; and about the expression of his face was a peace and a sweetness which seemed as a light shining from within.

"Great and noble in his life, he was greater and nobler in his death. There was about it a calmness, a recollection, a majesty, an order of perfect fitness and preparation worthy of the chamber of death, and such as became the last hours of a Pastor and Prince of the Church of God. He was a great Christian in all the deepest, largest, simplest, meaning of the name; and a great Priest in thought, word, and deed, in the whole career of his life, and in the mould of his whole being. He died the death of the just, making a worthy and proportionate end to a course so great.

"We have lost a Friend, a Father, and a Pastor, whose memory will be with us while life lasts. As one who knew him well, said well of him, 'We are all lowered by his loss.' We have all lost somewhat which was our support, our strength, our guidance, our pattern, and our pride. We have lost him who, in the face of this great people, worthily presented the greatness and the majesty of the Universal Church. He has fallen asleep in the midst of the generous, kindly, just, noble-hearted sympathy of the people, the public men, the public voices of England; a great people, strong and bold in its warfare, but humane, chivalrous and Christian to the antagonists who are worthy to contend with it. He is gone, but he has left behind him in our memories a long line of historical pictures, traced in the light of other days upon a field which will retain its colours fresh and vivid for ever. Some of you remember him as the companion of your boyhood, upon the bare hills of Durham; some in the early morning of his life, in the Sanctuaries of Rome; some see before them now his slender stooping form, on a bright winter's day, walking to the Festival of S. Agnes, out of the walls: some again, drawn up to the full stature of his manhood rising above the storm and contending with calm commanding voice of reason against the momentary excitement of the people of England. Some again can see him vested and arrayed as a Prince of the Church, with the twelve Suffragans of England closing the long procession which opened the first Provincial Synod of Westminster, after the silence of three hundred years. Some will picture him in the great hall of a Roman palace surrounded by half the Bishops of the world, of every language and of every land, chosen by them as their chief to fashion their words in declaring to the Sovereign Pontiff, their filial obedience to the Spiritual and Temporal power with which God has invested the Vicar of his Son. Some will see him feeble in death, but strong in faith, arrayed as a Pontiff, surrounded by the Chapter of his Church by word and deed verifying the Apostles' testimony, 'I have fought a good fight, I have finished my course, I have kept the faith,' and some will cherish above all these visions of greatness and of glory, the calm, sweet countenance of their best, fastest, friend and father lying in dim light of his chamber, not of death, but of transit to his crown. These things are visions, but they are substance. 'Transit gloria mundi' as the flax burns in fire. But these things shall not pass away. Bear him forth, Right Reverend Fathers and dear brethren in Jesus Christ—bear him forth to the green burial ground on the outskirts of this busy wilderness of men. It was his desire to die and to be buried, not amid the glories of Rome, but in the midst of his flock, the first Cardinal Archbishop of Westminster. Lay him in the midst of that earth, as a shepherd in the midst of his sheep, near to the Holy Cross, the symbol of his life, work, and hope; where the Pastors he has ordained will be buried one by one in a circle round about him in death, as they laboured round about him in life. He will be in the midst of us still. His name, his form, his words, his patience, his love of souls, to be our law, our rebuke, our consolation. And yet not so: it is but the body of this death which you bear forth with tears of loving veneration. He is not here. He will not be there. He is already where the Great Shepherd of the sheep is numbering His elect, and those who led them to the Fold of Eternal Life. And the hands which have so often blessed you, which anointed you, which fed you with the Bread of Life, are already lifted up in prayer, which never ceases day or night for you, one by one, for England, for the Church in all the world."

When the Right Rev. gentleman had concluded his beautiful discourse, the precatory Absolutions were chaunted by the prelates and clergy. This part of the ceremonies was performed by four prelates who have received episcopal consecration from the late Cardinal's hands. The absolutions had been arranged by the Rev. Dr. Crookall, from the music in the Papal chapel at Rome. The music was most solemn and impressive, and eminently befitting the occasion; and by the three hundred voices of priests and prelates it was rendered with imposing effect. Bishop Morris gave the final absolution, and with the chaunting of the "Requiescat in Pace," the most solemn function which the Catholic Church has celebrated in England since the "Reformation" was brought to a conclusion.

The celebrant clergy then quitted the church; and after the Rev. Dr. Gilbert, who had superintended all the ceremonies with untiring zeal, and an anxiety and earnestness trying to the strongest mental and physical energy, had announced the order of the funeral procession, the clergy and several religious bodies proceeded to their carriages; and the coffin was borne out by four laymen. So enormous was the crowd that these arrangements occupied nearly two hours, and it was nearly three o'clock before the funeral procession began to move away from the front of the church.

The following was the order of

THE FUNERAL CORTEGE.

Three Horsemen to keep the route of the funeral procession open.
Mourning Carriages, with Acolytes, Cross bearer, and Masters of the Ceremonies.
Sixty Mourning Coaches, each drawn by four black horses, containing the clergy of Westminster and Southwark, of Salford, Birmingham, and other dioceses, and members of the various Religious Orders already mentioned, clad in their sacerdotal or monastic robes.
Carriages immediately preceding the mortuary car:

FIRST CARRIAGE.

Very Rev. Canon John Walker.
Very Rev. Dr. Russell, of Maynooth College.
Very Rev. Canon Edward Hearn, D.D., the Cardinal's Vicar-General.

SECOND CARRIAGE.

Rev. Canon John Morris, of St. James', Spanish Place.
Rev. Canon Frederick Oakley, of St. John's, Duncan Terrace.
Very Rev. Monsignore Canon Francis Searle, the Cardinal's Secretary.
Rev. Canon William Weathers, D.D., of St. Edmund's College, Old Hall Green.

THIRD CARRIAGE.

Very Rev. Canon James O'Neal, Vicar-General, of St. John's Wood.
Rev. Canon George Last, of Ingatestone Hall.
Rev. Canon William Hunt, of St. James', Spanish Place.
Rev. Canon John Maguire, D.D., of Manchester Square.

The Bishops of England,
(all of whom were present except the Bishop of Hexham and
Newcastle, prevented by the state of his health from undertaking so long a journey) viz.:—

FOURTH CARRIAGE.
Right Rev. Monsignore Manning, Provost of Westminster.
Right Rev. Robert Cornthwaite, Bishop of Beverley.
Right Rev. Francis Kerril Amherst, Bishop of Northampton.
Right Rev. and Hon. William Clifford, Bishop of Clifton.

FIFTH CARRIAGE.
Right Rev. William Vaughan, Bishop of Plymouth.
Right Rev. Alexander Goss, Bishop of Liverpool.
Right Rev. Richard Butler Roskell, Bishop of Nottingham.
Right Rev. James Brown, Bishop of Shrewsbury.

SIXTH CARRIAGE.
Right Rev. William Turner, Bishop of Salford.
Right Rev. Thomas Grant, Bishop of Southwark.
Right Rev. William Bernard Ullathorne, Bishop of Birmingham.
Right Rev. Thomas Joseph Brown, Bishop of Menevia and Newport.

SEVENTH CARRIAGE.
Right Rev. William Bernard Allen Collier, Bishop of Drusipara.
Right Rev. Anthony O'Regan, Bishop of Dora.
Right Rev. William Wareing, Bishop of Retimo.
Right Rev. William Placid Morris, O.S.B., Bishop of Troy.

Carriage and six, containing the Very Rev. Mgr. Boone, Private
Chamberlain of His Holiness, bearing the Cardinal's Hat on a
cushion of cloth of gold, with the mantles of the three Equestrian
Orders conferred on His Eminence—namely, the Grand Cross of
the Sovereign Order of St. John of Jerusalem, the Grand Cross of
the Order of Charles III. of Spain, and the Grand Cross of the
Order of St. Januarius, of Naples, supported on both sides by Sir
George Bowyer, Bart., Knight of Precept of the Order of St. John
of Jerusalem, and Edmund Waterton, Esq., Chamberlain of Cape
and Sword of His Holiness.

THE BODY.

Borne on an open car (decorated with black and silver hangings,
surmounted by a celestial crown, and having immortelles at each
corner) drawn by six horses, the coffin being covered with a pall of cloth
of gold, bearing the Cardinal's arms.
Twelve Attendants, with Crape Armlets, and Cardinal's
Monogram on Medallion.
Relatives, Executors, Medical Men, and Solicitors, in Three Mourning
Coaches and Four.

FIRST CARRIAGE.
Rev. W. Burke, Mr. Burke, Mr. N. Wiseman, and Mr. Justice Shee.

SECOND CARRIAGE.
Monsignore Thompson, Rev. J. Bagshawe, Dr. Munk, and Mr. C.
Hawkins.

THIRD CARRIAGE.

Mr. Tegart, Mr. Tegart, jun., Mr. Harting, and Mr. Bagshawe.

Mourning Coach and Four, containing Mr. Newman and Mr. Roper, of the Cardinal's Household.

In another Carriage were the Right Hon. Mr. Justice O'Hagan, Dr. O'Connor, and Mr. William O'Connor.

The Cardinal's Private Carriage.

Mourning coaches with deputation from the Benevolent Society.

Mourning coach with members of the Aged Poor Society.

Mourning coaches with members of the Society of St. Vincent de Paul.

Carriage of the ex-Queen of the French.

Carriage of the Austrian Ambassador.

Carriage of the French Ambassador.

Carriage of the Greek Ambassador.

Private Carriages.

Of the private carriages it would be an impossibility in our limited space, to give a list. They numbered upwards of two hundred, including the carriages of the Catholic and Protestant noblemen and others mentioned above. It was the longest funeral procession, perhaps, ever seen in London, and some notion of its character may be formed when we mention that it occupied, from the first carriage to the last, a length of two miles. After the first mourning coaches had left the Cathedral fully an hour and a half elapsed before the last carriage followed.

The arrangements made by the police authorities were admirable; and it was well it was so, for the crowds of people who thronged the streets were so great that much confusion, and perhaps injury to life and limb, might have ensued, if timely provision had not been made. From the Cathedral to the end of the Marylebone Road there were eight hundred policemen ranged to keep the gazing crowds in order. And a stranger, unacquainted with London, and the vast list of mortality it holds within its embraces, would have been puzzled to know where all the people came from.

As the funeral procession moved from the Cathedral through South Place, Finsbury Place, and into Finsbury Square, the roadway was so crowded with people that the carriages had some difficulty in passing, and the police had as much as they could do to make a passage clear through the pressing crowd. The procession moved along the City Road; and here the crowds who lined each side of the way were as great, whilst every window of every house along the way had its gazing occupants. To avoid a portion of the route of the dense city traffic, the funeral procession turned down Old Street; and yet, though this was out of the expected line of route, the way was as thronged as if all Clerkenwell had turned out (as it must very nearly have done) to behold the strange and unaccustomed sight. Up Goswell Road, and into the Pentonville Road, the crowds were as great; and, in place of diminishing, they seemed to increase and thicken at King's Cross and along the Euston Road. Along the Marylebone Road the crowds were as great. In fact, for four miles and a half of the line of route every street and road was crowded with people. There could not have been less than one million of spectators to that funeral procession.

THE INTERMENT AT ST. MARY'S CEMETERY.

As early as three o'clock many hundred persons who were provided with tickets assembled at St. Mary's Cemetery, Kensal Green; but it was not till five o'clock that the body and the chief mourners arrived at the gates, which were besieged by such an immense multitude as to render the entrance to the cemetery somewhat difficult of approach. Owing to the cemetery being a private one, belonging to the Catholic Clergy of Westminster and Southwark, there was some technical difficulty in obtaining the services of the Metropolitan police to preserve order in it. This was, however, effectually done by a body of volunteers from the eastern districts of London, under the able guidance of their respected pastors, the Rev. W. Kelly and the Rev. D. Toomey. It is due to these good Catholic men to say that they did their duty firmly but gently.

The procession was formed, headed by the cross between acolytes, and followed by the regular and secular clergy and dignitaries of the church. This mournful train walked slowly, singing the Miserere to the solemn Gregorian Chant, towards the vault which had been prepared in the very centre of the plot appropriated for the interment of the London Catholic clergy. This spot was chosen, it is said, by the Cardinal Archbishop himself, who desired in death to be surrounded by those who had been his faithful and devoted sons on earth, and his able coadjutors in effecting the great changes in the religious feature of the Catholic body in the metropolis during the last sixteen years. An enclosure of white and black drapery, relieved by Latin and Maltese crosses, had been erected around the grave, and within this hallowed spot the Bishops and their immediate attendants entered. The chant of the "Miserere" was now followed by the sublime and deeply moving chorus of the "Benedictus," sung alternately by the chanters and the whole body of the clergy, which resounded through the solemn evening air with a most impressive effect. The last absolution over the grave was pronounced by the Right Rev. Bishop Brown of Newport, the senior Bishop present.

It is impossible to describe the beautiful solemnity of this most touching scene at this point—the dim evening light—the purple robes and white albs of celebrant prelates and priests—the sublime Gregorian chants sung by four hundred voices—the glare of those four hundred tapers—the coffin—the grave—and the hushed and attentive multitude around: words cannot convey a tithe of the sublime beauty of a scene like this. Strangers to the Catholic ritual who were present said in our hearing—"This, indeed, looks like the beauty of Christian worship." The crowd were silent—the officers on duty bowed their heads—the soldiers of the Royal Guards lifted up their caps— and the solemn chant of the four hundred united voices floated softly through the evening air; and then the coffin which contained the mortal remains of England's great Cardinal was consigned to its lowly dwelling, amid the whispered prayers of sorrowing thousands.

The spot where the great Cardinal of England—the first Archbishop of Westminster—the restorer of the Catholic hierarchy—the powerful expounder of the faith—the impressive preacher of its doc-

trine and morality—the father of the orphan and the poor—now rests,
is at present covered with a plain stone slab;—but ere long will be
seen, pointing heavenwards, a magnificent, and truly Christian mauso-
leum, which shall mark to future ages the spot where lies interred, in
the midst of his faithful flock—sheep and lambs—the mortal remains of

NICHOLAS CARDINAL WISEMAN,
FIRST ARCHBISHOP OF WESTMINSTER.

Requiescat in pace.

Amen!

LIST OF CARDINAL WISEMAN'S LITERARY WORKS.

Horæ Syriacæ seu Commentationes et Anecdota, Res vel Literas
  Syriacas Spectantia.—1828.
Two Lectures delivered in Rome—1831.
La sterilità delle missioni intraprese dai Protestanti per la conver-
  sione dei popoli infideli dimostrata delle relazioni degli stessi
  interassati nella medessima disertazione.—1831.
Two Lectures on Some Parts of the Controversy concerning 1 John
  v. 7.—1835.
Lectures on the Connection between Science and Revealed Religion.
  2 vols.—1836.
Lectures on the Principal Doctrines of the Catholic Church.—1836.
Letters to John Poynder, Esq., on his "Popery in Alliance with
  "Heathenism."—1836.
The Real Presence of the Body and Blood of our Lord Jesus Christ
  in the Blessed Eucharist proved from Scripture.—1836.
Funeral Oration on Cardinal Weld.—1837.
A Reply to the Rev. Dr. Turton's "Roman Catholic Doctrine of the
  Eucharist Considered." Philalethes in Cantabrigiensis, The British
  Critic, and the Church of England Quarterly Review.—1839.
Four Lectures on the Offices and Ceremonies of Holy Week, as per-
  formed in the Papal Chapels.—1839.
A Letter on Catholic Unity Addressed to the Earl of Shrewsbury.
  1841.
The Lamp of the Sanctuary, a Tale.
Remarks on a Letter from the Rev. Wm. Palmer.
Lectures on Religious Subjects, chiefly Doctrinal, delivered at St.
  Mary's, Moorfields.—1848.
A Sermon (on Luke x. 29), delivered on Sunday morning, 11th
  August, 1850.
A Sermon (on Luke x. 23-24), delivered on Sunday evening, August
  11th, 1850.
A Sermon (on Numbers i. 19-32) preached on behalf of the Aged
  Poor Society of London.—12th Dec., 1847-48.
An Appeal to the Reason and Good Feeling of the English people on
  the Subject of the Catholic Hierarchy.—1850.
Three Lectures on the Catholic Hierarchy.—1850.

The Social and Intellectual State of England compared with its Moral Condition. A Lecture.—1830.

Essays on Various Subjects.—3 vols.—1853.

On the Connection between the Arts of Design and the Arts of Production. A Lecture.—1853.

A Sermon (on 2 Cor. 12-9) delivered at Rome on the festival of St. Thomas of Canterbury.—29th Dec., 1853-54.

Four Advent Lectures on Concordats.—1855.

The future Historian's View of the present War.—1855.

Fabiola, or the Church in the Catacombs.—1855.

On the Influence of Words on Thought and Civilization. A Lecture. —1856.

An Account of some Explorations made in the Garden of the great Convent attached to the Church of Santa Sabina, Rome. Read before the Royal Society of Literature, June 25, 1856, and published in vol. 5, part 3 of its transactions.

"The Perpetuity of the Faith." A Sermon.—1856.

On the Nature of an Inaugural Discourse. An Introductory Lecture. —1856.

On the Perception of Natural Beauty by the Ancients and Moderns. Two Lectures.—1856.

Panegyric of St. Philip Neri.—1856.

Recollections of the Four Last Popes, and of Rome in their Times.— 1858.

The Hidden Gem; a drama in two acts; composed for the College Jubilee of St. Cuthbert's, Ushaw.—1858.

Tour in Ireland. Sermons and Lectures.—1859.

Hymn of St. Casimir to the B. Virgin, translated in same metre as original.

Hymnus in honorem Sti. Edmundi.—1860.

Inaugural Discourse pronounced at the First Meeting of the Academy of the Christian Religion.—June 29th, 1861.

A few Flowers from the Roman Campagna, in prose and verse.—1861.

Rome and the Catholic Episcopate : in reply to an Address of the Clergy to Cardinal Wiseman.—1862.

Points of Contact between Science and Art. A Lecture.—1863.

Judging from the Past and the Present, what are the prospects for good Architecture in London? A Lecture.—1864.

The Religious and Social Position of Catholics in England. An Address delivered to the Catholic Congress of Malines, Aug. 21st., 1863.—1864.

Sermons on Our Lord and His Blessed Mother.—1864.

Sermons on Moral Subjects.—1864.

William Shakspeare. A Lecture.—1865.

Nearly One Hundred Pastoral Letters and Lenten Indults.

And the following, which had been prepared for the Press by the late Cardinal, and will be published in the course of the year:

Sermons on the Doctrines of the Catholic Church.

Sermons on the Saints and Servants of God.

Meditations.—2 vols.

Cardinal Wiseman has left a large number of unpublished MSS., which it is hoped will one day be given to the public.

THE PRESS ON THE DEATH OF CARDINAL WISEMAN.

THE following extracts from the leading journals of the kingdom, which stand out in strong contrast with the opinions of the same writers in 1850-1, will, it is hoped, be thought worthy of a place at the close of this Memoir, as a record of the change of feeling towards His Eminence which has affected public writers since that period, for truly this is "a change of the right hand of the Most High":—

THE STAR.—"We have dwelt upon the great political and religious crisis which sprang up on the coming of Cardinal Wiseman, because it is mainly in connection with that crisis that England will remember the distinguished ecclesiastic who now lies dead. He came in storm; he has passed away in quiet. We do not say that his manner of coming was free from offence, but once installed it cannot be denied that he demeaned himself so as to discourage the revival of ill-feeling in the country. Despite the strange blending of nationalities represented in his parentage, birth, and education, Cardinal Wiseman was essentially an Englishman at heart. He was indeed thoroughly a man of the world, a courteous polished gentleman, a brilliant writer and speaker, an accomplished linguist. He was fond of society, and made friends and intimates among men of all parties and creeds. He loved art and the more elegant branches of literature. He represented his Church in her more showy, brilliant, and social character—as she is when she mingles with society and takes a quiet but active part in politics, and patronises art and loves pomp, and sustains the idea of hierarchial grandeur. Protestants as well as Catholics can well afford to bear cordial testimony to the great abilities, the varied acquirements, the high character, and, where private intercourse was concerned, the entirely liberal sentiments of Cardinal Wiseman. It was his misfortune, and ours, that he should have been introduced to the British public as the first English Cardinal of the modern era. But all must alike admit that he bore himself amongst us like a gentleman and a scholar; and all must surely regret to hear of the death of one who had so many splendid intellectual qualities and so many exalted and Christian virtues."

THE DAILY TELEGRAPH.—"Throughout the whole of England the news of Cardinal Wiseman's death will be received with sincere regret. Protestants and Catholics alike will combine in doing honour to the memory of a man who filled no unimportant post in our community, and filled it worthily. In every chapel of this country, where the ancient faith is still maintained, prayers have been offered up, during the last few weeks, for the restoration of health to the dying Cardinal. That those prayers were not answered is to all Englishmen —no matter what may be their creed—a source of real sorrow. A man of kindly nature, ripe learning, and genial disposition, he was known chiefly as an eloquent preacher and a scholar-like author. His portly figure, his pleasant smile, and jovial, good-humoured face accorded ill with the popular delusion which represents all priests of the Church of Rome as ascetic fanatics or Machiavellian intriguers. Emphatically a man of the world, he knew how to hold his place without arrogant pretension or any loss of real dignity in a society which did not recognise his rank. Though his appointment to the Catholic Archbishopric of Westminster gave rise to the storm of public indignation, he avoided every occasion of offending English feeling by the ostentation of authority. Cardinal Wiseman was a devout and zealous son of the Church; but he was also an author of some merit, a musician of more than ordinary talent, and, unless report was grossly mistaken, a man fond in moderation of social pleasures. Thus, through many points of his character, he was brought into contact with those who differed from him on the subject of religion, and the contact was beneficial for the priest as well as for the man. It was not that he loved Rome less, but that he loved England more. He had lived too long in the land which was almost that of his birth, not to be an Englishman rather than a foreigner."

THE MORNING ADVERTISER.—"Apart altogether from the high position which Cardinal Wiseman filled as the head of the Roman Catholic Church in the United Kingdom, he was a man whose varied information, great scientific attainments, and general literary acquisitions would have made him a person of mark in any of the learned professions. His style was regarded by many as a model of good taste; and several of his published works will, from the ability and literary taste they display, enjoy a lasting popularity. In private life he was an agreeable companion, and his society was sought by persons whose religious views did not harmonise with his."

THE TIMES.—"His memory will be looked back upon with feelings of greater interest and even admiration, than might have been thought possible from the prominent part he took in arousing one of the keenest religious discussions of this generation. In learning, in benevolence, and piety, it will be long ere the English Roman Catholic hierarchy can expect again to find the like of Nicholas Cardinal Wiseman."

THE PALL MALL GAZETTE, in an article unfavourable to the Cardinal, still renders justice to his merits:—"Cardinal Wiseman died this morning. His name will hereafter rank high among those ecclesiastics who have fought, under great difficulties, the battle of the Roman Church, and achieved great and unexpected, if not permanent, results. . . . The existing fabric of the Roman Church in England is, nevertheless, *a great fact*, whether destined to endure or not. Should this experiment fail, we may rest assured that no other will succeed. And it may fairly be predicted of the Cardinal's posthumous reputation that he will be recognised hereafter as the man who could have restored Catholicity in England, if its restoration had been possible."

THE SUN.—"Abroad, but more particularly in all the Catholic countries, in Italy, in France, in Belgium, and in Spain especially, the announcement of the death of Cardinal Wiseman will have been received with profound regret. His reputation was more than European. He was conspicuous for more than merely rare abilities. He was endowed with more than simply a capacious and vigorous intellect. He was a man of genius. As a great linguist, as a ripe scholar, as a man of profound learning, Cardinal Wiseman was a personage of mark and distinction even in an age when, among the holders of the same princely dignity, were numbered such giants of erudition and of philology as Cardinal Mai and Cardinal Mezzofanti. On the Continent, as our contemporary the *Morning Post* of to-day remarks, and with reason, he was regarded as a great man. It was only the other day that one of the very foremost intellects of our age—allusion being here made to the Rev. John Henry Newman—took occasion, in his famous *Apologia pro vita sua* to speak of Cardinal Wiseman in terms expressive of the highest admiration and veneration—words that, coming from a man like Dr. Newman, were of themselves an enviable panegyric. How completely Cardinal Wiseman had conquered the good opinion of his fellow-countrymen and fellow-citizens, here in England, during the fifteen years that have elapsed since the formation of the Catholic Hierarchy, of which, since 1850, the deceased Cardinal was, until yesterday, the head or spiritual chief as ' Archbishop of Westminster,' the opinions now being expressed upon all hands by the journalists of England afford a very signal and significant indication! These spontaneous and earnest opinions are of themselves in their way, no less distinctly a panegyric than the notable allusions already referred to as occurring so very recently in the pages of ' Newman's Apologia.' The angry feelings evidenced in 1850, are, in truth past and done with, long ago! And the fact that it is so is of itself an attestation of the singular combination in the late Chief of the Roman Catholic Church in England—of a dignity and a discretion, capable, by their conciliatory influence in their combination, of conquering all prejudices, even those that appeared to be the most rooted and ineradicable. Even in England, Cardinal Wiseman was a popular man. Among his co-religionists he was beloved and revered. But, apart from them, in the midst of the general public, in assemblages of Protestants and Dissenters, the deceased Cardinal was always of late years received with the respect due alike to his learning and to his virtues. It was only a very few years since, upon the occasion of the Canonization of the Japanese Martyrs, that—upon the gathering together, at Rome, of Catholic Bishops and Archbishops from the ends of the earth, to the number, hitherto unprecedented, of 400 wearers of the mitre—Cardinal Wiseman found upon his arrival in the Eternal City that the chair of the Presidency of the small and carefully selected inner council or committee, chosen from among those four hundred Bishops, Archbishops, and Cardinals, thus gathered together there at Rome, from all the countries of the world, had been reserved for himself! It was even more recently than that, that our leading contemporary the *Times* contained, as many may yet remember, a leading article, in which the probabilities (as it appeared to them) of Cardinal Wiseman's elevation to the Pontifical Throne under the style and title of Pope Pius X., were seriously discussed. Incidents—these two last mentioned—clearly indicative of the estimation in which, during his lifetime, Cardinal Wiseman was held both abroad and in England."

THE COURT JOURNAL.—" The death of Cardinal Wiseman has been recorded with an amount of eulogy of his character from Protestant journals which, to his friends and co-religionists, must have been extremely gratifying. No doubt he was a man amply fitted for the most arduous task that he had to'go through with in the introduction of Catholic religious power into this country. He followed out principles of conciliation, and being a genial, kind-hearted man, of refined, of literary, and of artistic tastes, his personal success in society smoothed over the asperities which might have resulted from the appointment of a man of a different disposition and tastes."

THE EXAMINER.—" To the London world and to the public at large Cardinal Wiseman's name was rendered most familiar by his frequent appearance upon the platform as a public lecturer upon a wide range of subjects connected with education, history, art, and science ; and in this capacity his Eminence always found an attentive and eager audience, even among those who were most conscientiously opposed to his spiritual claims. It is almost superfluous to add that his loss will be severely felt among the English Catholics, both lay and clerical, as he was nearly the only member of their body who had earned for himself a wide and lasting reputation for ability and learning for his gallant and meritorious conduct."

JOHN BULL.—" It must be allowed that the bearing of the Cardinal under the storm of popular indignation (in 1850), at least put his reputation for moral courage on a high eminence. Nor did the feelings thus evoked, cause any estrangement in his own mind, towards the people among whom he lived. He was to the last a popular lecturer and a favourite preacher, and his comparative early death will be felt by all, even the most sturdy Protestant among us as a national loss."

THE LONDON REVIEW.—" The distinguished ecclesiastic who has just passed away from among us will be long remembered as a man of cultivated tastes and accomplished mind—amiable and sociable in his temper, and naturally shrinking from public controversy and agitation—and yet who caused an outburst of national indignation and resentment in England which has had no parallel since the days of the Popish plot."

THE QUEEN.—" We are convinced that all just persons will agree with us when we declare that a Christian gentleman and a most ripe and cultivated scholar has been lost to the world. Cardinal Wiseman died after a lingering illness in the sixty-third year of his age. He was, indeed, a most accomplished linguist, as well as a very profound scholar."

BELL'S WEEKLY MESSENGER.—" The skill with which the Cardinal avoided controversy was scarcely less remarkable than the vigour he displayed when it was forced upon him. He could reply with dignity to such divines as Dr. Turton and Dr. Whittaker, but he treated with becoming silence the numerous Clergymen who attempted to make theological capital out of him. These attempts were frequently scurrilous enough, and one London doctor who did not understand why the Cardinal's letters were dated from the Flaminian Gate, 'commended him to his home on the Flaminian way.' "

CHURCH TIMES.—" The death of Cardinal Wiseman is peculiarly a loss to the Roman Church in England, but those who knew his Eminence in the neutralised world of letters speak of him with respect and esteem as a learned scholar, of refined mind, and a kindly, genial disposition. He ruled the hierarchy with a light but firm hand, and, in its present circumstances, the choice of his successor will be a work of some difficulty."

THE PATRIOT (leading organ of the Dissenters).—" The lying-in-state of a Prince of the Holy Roman Church—the Cardinal Archbishop of Westminster—in the metropolis of Protestantism, is suggestive of many reflections, and illustrates strikingly the liberty which Protestants can allow as well as enjoy. The freedom which we claim we give ; and no man has ever made fuller trial of our tolerance than the able ecclesiastic whose remains are this day attended to their last resting-place with almost royal pomp and state. Cardinal Wiseman has for the last thirty years been one of the most prominent men in England, and has occupied a position and wielded an influence which no foreign-born priest could have enjoyed. Cardinal Wiseman, with all his faults,—perhaps we might say, in his faults,—was a thorough Englishman ; and though he committed himself deeply to the Ultramontane doctrine and spirit, there was something in his English culture and full communion with English life which tempered his Ultramontane zeal, and made him a very different man from the popular notion of a Papal emissary. A certain humane influence was shed over his life, not so much by his high intellectual culture as by his reputation for general learning, and which he was unwilling to risk by any acts or utterances of bigotry which would have shocked the sense of the English people. His learning was of that showy, brilliant kind which is most useful to the rhetorician, though it was very far from superficial. But the reputation for refined scholarship, when cherished, acts as a softening, subduing medium, and tends to tone down the harshness of religious bigotry and polemical strife. To the last, Cardinal Wiseman prided himself with justice on his scientific and æsthetic attainments ; and one of the very last, if not the last occasion on which he appeared in public, showed him to be no mean critic of the various styles of architecture, and no mean proficient in the history of the art. These tastes and pursuits formed a link of connection between the Prince of the Roman Church and free minded, free-spoken Englishmen, which no mere narrow-minded foreign zealot could have established ; and they gave him a large audience of intelligent and cultivated Protestants whenever he appeared before the public. He was a preacher of varied and highly-cultivated powers. His word-painting was masterly, and he used it lavishly. The range of topics and the mode of treatment which are imposed by the necessities of their position on the preachers of the Roman Church, are specially favourable to rhetoricians ; and of these the late Cardinal Archbishop was among the chief. His style was turgid, and had a foreign flavour; still it was very powerful for the purpose for which he used it. The Church of Rome has few men left who are capable of handling with ability and power so large a range of subjects, and of making the position and influence of a Roman priest a thing of power outside the pale of the Roman Church. None have questioned the simplicity and sincerity of his faith; and when he said in dying, that "he felt like a child going home," something reveals itself, which, happily, belongs exclusively neither to the Roman nor the Protestant world of thought and experience. We feel the touch of nature which makes the whole world kin, and can join very heartily in the pious ejaculation which myriads will utter this day over his grave, "May he rest in peace."

MANCHESTER EXAMINER.—"Since 1850 the history of Cardinal Wiseman has been, just what it might have been expected to be, that of an accomplished scholar and a devoted Prelate. The hours which he has been able to snatch from his ecclesiastical duties have been given to literary pursuits. More has been done by his pen to elevate the English literature of the Catholic Church than by any author since the Reformation. As a specimen of his versatility, it may be mentioned, that what may be called his representative works are, 'Horæ Syriacæ,' 'Science and Revealed Religion,' 'History of the Last Four Popes,' 'Fabiola,' and the 'Hidden Gem,'—'Fabiola' being a novel of great excellence, and the 'Hidden Gem' a religious drama of a modern kind. It is no discredit to the Cardinal, to say that what may be called his happiest efforts were in his short translations. He has left many of these behind him; and one of them will ever have a peculiar interest. It is inscribed upon a piece of plate, which he has left as an heir-loom to his successors. This relic bears the figure of Our Saviour giving his charge to Peter. His Eminence told the Bishops, at a recent meeting in London, that he had bequeathed it to his successor, and that he wished it to be preserved as a memorial of their councils. The following Latin inscription engraved upon it, as well as the translation, are by the Cardinal himself:—

> ' Qui·Christi·Post·Me·Pascis·Me·Dignior·Agnos·
> Ipso·In·Smyposio·Sis·Memor·Officii·
> Nec·Dum·Te·Laute·Tractas·Socio·que·Beatos·
> Lazarus·Ante·Fores·Languet·Esuriens·'

[TRANSLATION.]

> ' Who, after me, more worthily, of Christ dost feed the sheep,
>   Remembrance of thy duty, even at the banquet keep;
> Nor when, for thee, with genial friends, the festive board is spread,
>   Let Lazarus, before thy door, sink for want of bread.'

The precept which the Cardinal thus bequeaths to his successor is one which he has always adopted himself. Whether regarded in his public character or in his private and ecclesiastical capacity, he leaves behind him a reputation which will be appreciated by men of all classes; nor will it be easy for the Church of which he was so distinguished an ornament to find a suitable successor."

HULL ADVERTISER.—" The greatest among the present generation of England's great men has ceased to be numbered with the living. Cardinal Wiseman rests from his many and exhausting labours, sleeping the sleep of a tranquil, peaceful, and episcopally exemplary death. Pre-eminent as a scholar and linguist among the greatest scholars and linguists of the nineteenth century—Europeanly famous among Divines for his knowledge of Canon Law and erudite familiarity with Holy Scripture in the oriental languages—distinguished among authors and artists for his really marvellously accurate acquaintance with the whole range of ancient and modern literature, science and art—and blessed with a capacity, a sweetness of temper, and a geniality of disposition which made his wonderful stores of erudition available for the instruction of men of all ranks, classes, climes, and creeds, Cardinal Wiseman occupied by general consent the foremost place among the intellectual luminaries of the age. Wherever he appeared, all unconsciously concurred in the all-pervading feeling that how many claimants soever there might be for the second place, the first of right belonged to him. By his death Pius IX. looses a wise Counsellor, the Catholic Church an illustrious Prelate, and Queen Victoria a great subject, who has contributed not a little to render her reign illustrious. For it need no longer be concealed that the Cardinal cordially sympathized—and not inactively or resultlessly—with the efforts of the late Prince Consort in the promotion of the exhibitive study of Art in England, and that the recognition of the value of that sympathy, made without the intervention of Cabinet Ministers, was to the Cardinal exceedingly gratifying. Cardinal Wiseman was a man of Herculean frame, but with a voice exceedingly gentle, and almost feminine in the clearness and sweetness of its lower tones. He was remarkably cheerful and animated in conversation, and had the happy art of conveying information, as if those he addressed had rather forgotten than never before heard it. He affected no reserve, treating all who approached him with an easy confidence, which at once gained the good will of strangers. It was impossible to know him for any length of time without observing that his early life had been spent innocently, and that he retained an extraordinary amount of the simplicity of childhood in his admiration of all that related to that happy period of life. There was a well spring of simple piety, and almost infantine goodness in the Cardinal of which nothing appeared to those who had not opportunities of looking below the surface. This was one of the secrets of his strength, of which he seemed himself unconscious. No man was ever less a plotter or a diplomatist than the Cardinal, on the contrary, he was as open and unreserved as John Bull himself; but he had faith in God and in the righteousness of the work in which he was engaged, and his moral courage in the highest order—that which would conduct a martyr calmly and even joyously to the block. For in good truth the Cardinal was a man to lay down his life for the faith which he professed."

SPIRITUAL MAGAZINE.—" We cannot allow the departure of this eminent prince of the Catholic Church to pass unnoticed, without a word of tribute to his high character. During his life it was perhaps difficult, if not impossible, from the prejudices, as well as from the reasonable objections of Protestant Christians against the aggressive nature of Roman Catholicism, that Cardinal Wiseman should obtain a just appreciation at the hands of his countrymen; but now that his life here has ended, and it can be seen in its completeness, it is very visibly one in which, as Englishmen and as Christians, we may take an honest pride, and be glad that he was one of us. The talents which he brought to bear on all of the many subjects which he studied, would do honour to any man, and his earnest Christian life and manful efforts for Catholicism, would be an ornament to any form of religious organization. If he was a true Catholic, also a true Christian was this good and great man. Englishmen will now do justice to the late Cardinal; and we feel sure that a wish will be realized to which he gave expression to a faithful friend, who is our informant, a few days before his departure, that "after he had gone some few would miss him, and that many good English Protestants would cease to think of him as a monster."

REV. DR. THOMAS, EDITOR OF THE HOMILIST.—"Occupying as Cardinal Wiseman did, a position in the Catholic Church second only to the Pope himself, he was an object around which the sympathies of millions of devout hearts gathered with reverence and awe. He was the prince of the Church of Rome in England, and to all the members of that Church on this island he was the spiritual master and guide. Since the death of Cardinal Pole, in the reign of Queen Elizabeth, three hundred years ago, no Cardinal had been buried in this country. [Cardinal Pole died on the same day as Queen Mary, and was buried in Canterbury Cathedral]. Hence the depth and expanse of that excitement which his death has produced. It was not improper for us to sympathise with our Catholic brethren in this hour of their distress. The Cardinal's death had left a perceptible blank in English society. His Eminence's theological and scientific attainments were great even for a prelate. Even ill-natured, hostile critics, high in their standard, severe in their scrutiny, such as the *Saturday Review*, paid respect to his attainments. He considered Governments ought to allow their subjects the utmost freedom in religious matters, and proceeded to call to mind the popular demand made upon the Government to interfere to prevent Dr. Wiseman from taking the title of Archbishop of Westminster. The less thoughtful pulpits of the land, both in and out of the Establishment, sought to alarm their flocks with horrid pictures of Popery, and of the danger of the Pope coming to England to take possession of Queen Victoria's throne. Platforms were reared in all parts of the kingdom where fanaticism and bigotry ran riot, and where speeches were delivered, which perhaps most of their authors would now blush to own. Even journalism in many cases, yielded to the influence of the excitement, and became the organs of the miserable spirit that prevailed. Nor in Parliament were there wanting those who echoed and advocated the claims of the uproarious bigotry of the time. In truth, it was a dangerous thing for a public man of that time not to go with that spirit."

EXTRACTS FROM THE CATHOLIC PRESS.

THE TABLET.—" That the end must come, that it was near at hand, and, at last, that nothing short of a miracle could prolong his life more than a few hours, was known to the Catholic Faithful and to the whole public before the solemn tidings came that on Wednesday, the 15th of February, the Feast of SS. Faustinus and Jovita, MM., at eight o'clock a.m., the great English Cardinal, the first Archbishop of Westminster, the champion and the chief, the glory and the pride, of the restored Church in England, had yielded up his soul to God. It is a great blow. It is an irreparable loss. But it would be a selfish and unworthy thought that would repine, or that would grudge his well-deserved reward to one who had toiled for God and for the Church of God so manfully and long. Well may men say of him, " Ecce sacerdos magnus!' He was a great Priest! Truly may they add, ' Non est inventus similis illi.' The like of him had not been seen amongst us, and we who have known him have little right to expect in our day to see his like again. What a giant he was in his towering intellectual superiority, in the immense impulsion of his strong will, in the free large play of his vast resources, in the grand scale of his designs, and in the elevation of his aims! He was one whom it was safe to trust and follow. And he was the easiest and most liberal of men. Whoever desired like himself the good and glory of the Spouse of Christ above all else, and was willing like himself to spend and be spent in Her service, was sure of the largest scope, of the freest range, of the kindliest welcome, of the readiest help. . . . It may be allowed to those who knew and loved the Man to advert with satisfaction to this proof of his great natural qualities, and it would be ungracious to advert to it without remembering that it is a vindication of the Cardinal's own unfailing reliance on the generosity of Englishmen, on the ultimate triumph over their prejudices, of their love of justice and fair play, and on their sympathy with manhood and with worth. The crowds who flocked daily to enquire after him during his last illness, the language of the Protestant press, and the general tone of society all attest, that Nicholas Cardinal Wiseman, the author of the Letter from without the Flaminian Gate, was one of the most popular of Englishmen. But that the Cardinal of St. Pudentiana should be known and understood, it would be necessary to venture upon more sacred ground, and to speak of the spiritual life of the great Archbishop, whom the ignorant and the malicious censured as worldly-minded, self-indulgent, fond of pomp and of display, a proud Prelate and an ambitious Ecclesiastic. There are those who can tell us of that wonderful maid-like purity, which was like a light around him from his boyhood's days, of his child-like faith, and of his intense devotion to the Heart of Jesus, to the Blessed Sacrament, to the Immaculate Mother of God, and how the affections of his heart, which overflowed towards his earthly friends, glowed with supernatural warmth towards his heavenly patrons. There was no subject in which he could not take an interest, and on which he could not at a moment's notice bring to bear a whole train of original ideas and unhackneyed illustrations; but there was no subject from which he would not gladly turn to converse with ten-fold interest on the report of a new miracle, the authentication of a doubtful relic, the foundation of a new convent, the letter of a foreign missionary, or the smallest details of an Ecclesiastical Rite. If ever man felt that the most trifling fact connected with the Divine Service, or referable to the Church of Christ, was intrinsically more valuable, and was dearer to him than the most important mundane matter, it was the celebrated scholar, the enthusiastic artist, the man of great achievements and of yet greater aims, Nicholas Wiseman, Cardinal Priest of the Holy Roman Church, and First Archbishop of Westminster."

WEEKLY REGISTER.—"A great bereavement long threatened may lose indeed the stunning effect of suddenness; but as the loss is made none the lighter by its tardy approach, so the grief can be none the less poignant. His loss is not ours alone, it is the loss of the whole world; of literature, art, civilisation and the Catholic Church. Never could it be more truly said—

> Quis desiderio sit pudor aut modus
> Tam cari capitis?
>
> Multis ille bonis flebilis occidit.

"Our greatest man has fallen a victim to that fatal stroke which awaits us all in our turn. A life of signal usefulness, of heroic self-sacrifice, and of brilliant success, has this week closed by a death not merely holy and edifying, but a death such as every true-hearted Prelate would wish to die—surrounded by every holy rite and canonical observance befitting not only the great faith and the undaunted ecclesiastical spirit but also the exalted rank of the sufferer. For many years past the declining health of the Cardinal Archbishop had from time to time caused great anxiety to his friends, his spiritual subjects, and to all who valued his precious life. From time to time severe and exhausting attacks of illness, and a series of most painful and hazardous surgical operations, were endured with heroic patience, and scarcely occasioned any intermission of His Eminence's labours for Religion and the Church. Still these successive attacks, and perhaps scarcely less the treatment which they necessitated, gradually reduced the Cardinal's strength, till one day of exposure, excitement, and over-exertion brought on at length that final seizure from which he never rallied. The day we allude to was the 6th of last December, the Feast of his holy patron, the great Bishop of Myra. His Eminence's great devotion to St. Nicholas is well known. It was by his own choice that he entered on that day into possession of his See on the Restoration of the English Hierarchy in 1850; but it was by no choice of his own—shall we call it a Providential dispensation, or a remarkable coincidence?—that on that same day he concluded his earthly ministrations, preached his last sermon, and gave for the last time that oft-imparted Episcopal Blessing to the Faithful. It was from the House of La Sainte Union, Highgate Rise, the last (or nearly the last) of the multitude of religious communities established in England under his auspices, that Cardinal Wiseman went home to die. . . . .

"Truly there was great fitness in the circumstance that he who has been Heaven's chosen instrument more than all other Prelates and missioners who have laboured in England as yet to reverse the work of sacrilege and apostacy that tore our country from the Faith, should himself exhibit, as in his life, so also in his death, a perfect model of Episcopal behaviour in all the details of ecclesiastical observance.

"It might easily have been otherwise, and without any cause for dissatisfaction. Many a Prelate of the Church has finished a career that had been both holy, and useful, and successful, without—in the closing scene itself—superadding to the edifying example of faith, hope, and charity, another also, and that an historical one of ecclesiastical dignity and almost liturgical exactness, at the supreme moment of life.

"We of the laity have much reason to thank our God that all has been as it has. We may confidently hope that our own prayers, offered at the Exposition of the XL Hours throughout the Archdiocese, that great devotion which he himself instituted and taught us, have prevailed with Heaven—if not for his recovery, yet for that which he himself desired far more ardently—his happy death.

"And now we feel oppressed and well-nigh overwhelmed with the duty which devolves upon us of writing some not too unworthy memorial of the illustrious deceased. What shall we say? The time is brief, there is no opportunity for research or meditation on so fruitful a theme. The personal and intimate friends of his Eminence, who could tell so much that the public would be eager to know, are too much absorbed in their own grief, or in the melancholy duties which the Cardinal Archbishop's demise has involved, to put pen to paper for us. The facts we have to recall are perhaps only such as they already know: the feelings we essay to express they also experience so acutely that even eloquence could hardly escape the reproach of inadequateness to utter them.

"Nothing comes more appositely to the recollection in recalling the words of genius upon a topic in some respects not dissimilar, than the lines of our great dramatist about the last Cardinal but one who lived and died on English ground. How real in their present application are the words that describe the brighter side of Wolsey's character and career; how opposite to our present subject are those which refer to its darker tints and the less happy points of his history!—

> ' This Cardinal,
> Though from a humble stock, undoubtedly
> Was fashioned to much honour. From his cradle
> He was a scholar, and a ripe and good one;
> Exceeding wise, fair-spoken, and persuading;
> Lofty and sour to those that loved him not;
> But to those men that sought him sweet as summer.
> And though he were unsatisfied in getting,
> Which were a sin, yet in bestowing,
> He was most princely. Ever witness for him
> Those twins of learning that he raised in you,
> Ipswich and Oxford, one of which fell with him,
> The other though unfinished yet so famous,
> So excellent in art and still so rising,
> That Christendom shall ever speak his virtue.
> His overthrow heaped happiness upon him,
> For then, and not till then, he felt himself
> And found the blessedness of being little:
> And to add greater honours to his age
> Than man could give him, he died fearing God.'"

UNIVERSAL NEWS.—" A Prince of the Church lies dead in the heart of London. A man whose talents were recognized and honoured wherever civilization spread its flag and reaped its conquests, is no more. Cardinal Wiseman occupied no unworthy place among his contemporaries. Contending with disadvantages which smite down ordinary men, and silence the voice of publicists who believe that the profession of faith is the road to ruin, he worked in this chief capital of heresy with a zeal, an exactitude, perseverance, an indomitable eagerness for triumph, that at last wrought the path to victory, and placed himself at the head of the turmoil as the conqueror. Other men, however gifted, honoured, and revered, would have fainted and fallen by the way in the deadly combat which he waged with irresistible courage against the fallacies of his time, and in defence of rights and principles which to him were as certain as the guarantees of his salvation. Even those who urged him on against the spring-tide of English opinion, when disaster threatened to fall upon the Church, and the nation rose like a man against what was ludicrously termed " Papal aggression," censured in the end the heroic stubbornness of heart and solidity of disposition with which he armed himself against the outcry of the nation, amazed and disquieted by the new attitude assumed by our Church in these kingdoms. His Eminence knew the task to which he was committed from its heights to its foundation. He was no simple expeditionist, but a man who had long reconnoitred the field that lay before him, and was resolved to accomplish the task to which he was apportioned. . . . .
Here was a man who carried his triumphs from battle-field to battle-field, armed only with the supreme consciousness of right, and the unconquerable love of truth. Churches were glad to hear him; not more so than learned societies, which he amazed, enlightened, and enraptured. The prince who celebrated mass yesterday, or, mounting the pulpit, poured forth one of those majestic utterances that, happily for the world, live in print, might be found to-day in the front of some magnificent assembly, asserting by his profound reflection and splendid intuitive powers, his right to an undisputed post amongst the chiefs and benefactors of humanity. Cardinal Wiseman was not only a profound scholar, but an acute and most intelligent observer. Facts which escaped the notice of ordinary men yielded up their secrets and influence to his keen analytical gaze. He was an ecclesiastic, but was, in addition, an explorer in the realms of research that lie outside the range of ecclesiastical functions. His scientific lectures of themselves would be sufficient to establish his claim to no unmerited place in the gallery of men whose hearts and souls, in the interests of science, were given, as Bacon observes, as ' hostages to fortune.'"

UNIVERSE.—" It is now, when our Cardinal Archbishop is gone, that his loss will be most severely felt by the Catholics, not by the diocese alone, but by all England. The question everywhere asked is, Who is to fill up the vast gap thus left in our ecclesiastical hierarchy? One is spoken of for his scholarship, another for his eloquence and talent, a third for his rank and piety, and others still for different gifts by which they are distinguished; but it is admitted on all hands that no one can be found in the English Church to fill the moral, social, and intellectual void caused by the death of his Eminence.

"The extent and accuracy of his information was almost incredible. In every department of literature, art, and science (natural as well as revealed) he was deeply versed, and his various works, lectures, essays, reviews, novels, poems, and plays, form a lasting monument of genius, as fertile as it was varied and exhaustless."

NORTHERN PRESS.—"Never was Cardinal Wiseman greater than amid the universal outcry against him; calmly and fearlessly he awaited the issue. The invective and opprobrium with which he was assailed are forgotten or obliterated, and we venture to say that no man in so short a space of time has succeeded in removing more difficulties, or in attaching to himself more sincere friends than the lamented Cardinal Wiseman. It was a brief but stormy episode in his remarkable life, and we are sure that Englishmen of all denominations will meet around his grave and breathe a prayer for his memory. Few men have attained to more celebrity—to him literature and science paid court, the most distinguished in the land feeling complimented and honoured with his acquaintance. As a devoted son of the Church, Cardinal Wiseman ever evinced towards her his love and devotion. Rome was his delight, it was the home of his heart, and around it were entwined all the sympathies and affections of his soul. Rome he loved as dearly in his decline as he did in the days of his boyhood, when, with all the enthusiasm of youth he listened to the tales that were told of the eternal city, and longed to set his foot upon that hallowed soil. As his youthful dreams were realised by a subsequent connection with the eternal city, so his wishes to witness the re-establishment of the English hierarchy were realised, and his dearest designs accomplished of gathering around him in his latest moments the defenders of the Holy See, and deputing to them the task he had left himself unaccomplished. Whilst among them, his labours in the vineyard were unceasing, and he is gone to enjoy his reward where toil and sorrow are no more. REQUIESCAT IN PACE."

From the "MONTH."

"THE FIRST ARCHBISHOP OF WESTMINSTER,
February 15th, 1865.

"The world affirms—a courtly gentleman,
In whom rich veins of classic culture ran,
Mixed with the varied learning of the time,
Adorned by Raffaele's brush, by Dante's rhyme,
Is gathered to the scholars gone before.
The man whom England will behold no more—
No taunt of alien on his ashes thrown !—
She's proud to claim to reckon as her own,
Proud even of the purple that he wore !
For he was great among her greatest men,
Famed and persuasive both with voice and pen ;
Stately in presence, kindly to behold,
And cast by nature in that ample mould
Of intellectual strength which wins the crown,
Admired by all men, of the world's renown.

" Wild as the wave that wars against a rock—
As firmly rooted to withstand the shock,
England and he a few short years ago !
But her stout hearts, however angered, know
How well to honour the unblenching foe
Who yet was more than friend !
                Let time declare
What kind of heart was that which lying there,
Pulseless and cold, knew not the crowd which prest
To touch with cross and bead his saintly breast,
To look their last upon his broad calm brow.
He, like a ' child from school,' gone homeward now,
Bearing all blessings which the Church can give
To those who die in Him by whom we live,
Asks only prayers which surely turn to praise
Before they reach the throne !   Let future days
Give more effectual honour, gathering more
Of the blest fruits of what he did and bore,
When the great empty fane which coldly rears
Its darkened roof above the waste of years,
Again shall open wide its western door
To the blest faith of Fisher and of More ;
And when men need no more by stealth to pray ;
Where Edward's suppliants wore the stones away ;
When Tudor Henry's fretted walls resound
With steps and voices meet for hallowed ground ;
When that chill altar shall regain the Guest,
Three centuries absent from His place of rest ;
When life and light shall banish night and death,
And the great Minster breathe with living breath,—
Men will remember that the rightful heir
To all the pious founders cherished there,
The first great Pastor of the name and throne,
Died as he lived—an exile from his own ;
That not for him did Henry's walls unclose—
That far from Edward's shrine his feet repose —
But they well know that though his ashes lie
In the green earth beneath the open sky,
The spiritual fabric by his hand restored
Was England's living temple to the Lord,
Within whose sacred bounds he rests in state,
PRIEST, PASTOR, BISHOP, FRIEND, and ADVOCATE !

                              B. R. P."